PLAY FOR KEEPS

BRENDA BARRETT

PLAY FOR KEEPS

A Jamaica Treasures Book/December2024
Published by Jamaica Treasures
Manchester, Jamaica

This is a work of fiction. Names, characters, places, and incidents are either the product of the author's imagination or are used fictitiously. Any resemblance to an actual person or persons, living or dead, events, or locales is entirely coincidental.

ISBN 978-976-97430-4-5

Jairo walked over to her and placed a plate of sandwiches in front of her. "What drink would you like with this? I've got a variety of options to choose from."

"I'll see what you have." Audra moved away from him and went toward the fridge door, pulling it open.

Jairo cornered her at the fridge door, trapping her between his body and the fridge. "I don't like you keeping me at arm's length."

"I, uh..." Audra swallowed. "Don't look at me like that and give me some space. Jason is in the next room."

Jairo chuckled. "I've been craving a kiss from you."

"We can't keep this up," Audra whispered, looking at his lips longingly. "It needs to stop. I can't think when you're so near."

"Move in with me," Jairo said. "I want to see you and Jason every day."

"No," Audra shook her head.

"I'll wear you down," Jairo said confidently.

"I doubt that." Audra exhaled when he moved away. She had been primed and ready for that kiss. It took a while for her pulse to stop thrumming like a car in overdrive. The man just had to look at her once to turn her into a wanton mess. She had to conquer this.

ALSO BY BRENDA BARRETT

FULL CIRCLE
NEW BEGINNINGS
THE PREACHER AND THE PROSTITUTE
AFTER THE END
THE EMPTY HAMMOCK
THE PULL OF FREEDOM
REBOUND SERIES
THREE RIVERS SERIES
NEW SONG SERIES
BANCROFT SERIES
MAGNOLIA SISTERS SERIES
SCARLETT SERIES
WILEY BROTHERS SERIES
PRYCE SISTERS SERIES
THE JACKSONS SERIES
CRIMSON HILL SERIES
SPICE AND STONE SERIES
RIDGEVIEW SERIES

ABOUT THE AUTHOR

Brenda Barrett is an award-winning and bestselling author who has a passion for writing real Jamaican romances.

When she's not weaving words that transport readers to exotic locales, you can find her nurturing her green thumb in the garden or doting on her beloved cats.

With an infectious zest for life, this author brings a unique perspective to her writing that is both relatable and thought-provoking.

Don't be surprised if you find yourself lost in the pages of her latest work, as she seamlessly blends romance with some drama, mystery, and suspense, or even sci-fi, leaving readers wanting more.

You can connect with Brenda online at:
Brenalbar.com
Twitter.com/AuthorWriterBB
Facebook.com/AuthorBrendaBarrett

Chapter One

It was raining heavily. Echoes of thunder rumbled in the background as lightning lit up the night sky. Audra jumped out of bed.

"I have to go home."

"Why?" her bed partner asked sleepily. "You might as well stay the night. It's late."

"No, I can't." Audra groaned. "I have responsibilities."

"What responsibilities?" He cracked an eye open.

"Uhm, work." Audra ran her fingers through her disheveled hair.

"You can't be serious," he murmured. "You work with your parents. You basically have a nine-to-five job."

"That is so not true! Sometimes I help out at the hospital. Unfortunately, there are always sick children who need my help," Audra said. "Where are my clothes?"

"All over the house," he murmured. "I started tearing them off you the moment I answered the door."

Audra groaned. "I'm going to do something about this."

"What?" he chuckled softly, sitting up in bed.

"See a psychiatrist," Audra said. "My mental health is unraveling. I can't keep doing this."

"We're not hurting anybody," he said. "You're still single, aren't you?"

"Yes," Audra hissed. She spotted her underwear near the door. She picked it up and looked at it; it was torn. She might as well bin it. Her blouse was similarly tattered, and her skirt on the stairwell looked a little worse for wear.

"I'm going to have to borrow one of your shirts," she said, turning around and heading for the closet. "My clothes are fit for the waste bin. Such a pity—I loved that blouse."

"I'll buy you a whole wardrobe," he said lazily. "I've been thinking we should formalize our situationship."

Audra shrugged into one of his shirts and turned around. The shirt could be a baggy dress; it would have to do. When she went home, she would sneak into the guest house, shower, and then collect Jason from her parents' house. It was a weeknight, after all. She only left Jason with them on weekends. They would wonder why she was getting home so late, and she didn't want to lie. What would she say? Mom, Dad, Jairo called, and as usual, I went running. Did someone have a prescription for what she had? She would happily take it. Her resistance to him was somewhere below zero.

"Audra, you didn't respond," he said huskily.

"Sorry," Audra said. "I was wondering how I was going to sneak in without my parents knowing."

"Why are you sneaking around?" He looked at her with narrowed eyes. "You're an adult, not a child. What are you hiding?"

"Nothing," Audra said. "I wonder if my shoes are still

intact?"

He chuckled. "Audra, can we have a serious conversation?"

Audra inhaled. "Are you going to put on clothes?"

"Okay," he said, getting up.

She averted her eyes. She found him irresistible naked. Then again, she found him irresistible with clothes on, too.

"Okay, all good," he said. "You can look now."

He had pulled on black track bottoms with a matching shirt.

"Can we go downstairs?" Audra asked. "Closer to my car?"

"Sure." He held the door while she passed him.

"Don't touch me," Audra said, her voice brittle.

"I won't," he sighed. "Believe it or not, I've come to the same conclusion you have, we're combustible together. I've never felt like this before. Makes me feel a little out of control."

Audra paused and looked at him. "That's good to know— that this malady isn't only infecting me."

Jairo chuckled. They headed downstairs and into the living room. Audra found her shoes and put them on.

He watched her silently, then said, "I bought a house."

Audra spun around. "Good. Congrats. That's how many houses now?"

"Thirteen," he answered solemnly. "The others are investments. This house I'm talking about is a personal residence—in Jamaica."

Audra looked at him incredulously. "Oh really?"

"Yes," Jairo nodded. "I was thinking I need to move back home, get settled, start a family."

Audra cleared her throat. "Well, that's nice."

"I guess we'll see more of each other," Jairo said.

"Uh-huh." Audra nodded.

"And it would stand to reason since we can't keep our hands off each other, that we should look into making things official," Jairo said.

"Official as in… married?" Audra asked, widening her eyes.

"I never want to get married again," Jairo shrugged. "It wasn't a fulfilling experience. I was thinking more along the lines of us moving in together. That way, you don't have to sneak off into the night."

"I'm not sneaking around," Audra said "just stealthily approaching the guest house without them seeing me."

"So, what do you say, Audra?" Jairo asked.

"I can't." Audra inhaled raggedly and headed to the front door. "I have a son. I want him to have an example of a stable, committed relationship. I don't want him growing up confused or feeling like things are temporary."

Jairo frowned, stepping closer. "When did you have a son? Why am I just finding out? How old is he?"

Audra inhaled. "He's eight."

"Eight!" Jairo looked at her in disbelief. "You had him while you were in college?"

"Final year," Audra said.

"Who is his father?" Jairo asked quietly.

Audra bit her lip. This was the moment of truth. If she blurted out you, things would forever change.

She hesitated, her heart racing. She could feel Jairo's eyes on her, waiting, expecting an answer. She had avoided this moment for years—the truth that would turn everything upside down.

She took a deep breath and finally met his gaze. "You," she whispered.

Jairo blinked, his expression unreadable. "What?" he asked, his voice low.

"You," Audra repeated, her voice firmer this time. "You're his father, Jairo."

Silence fell between them, thick and heavy. Jairo's face shifted from confusion to shock, then anger. "Why didn't you tell me? All these years—" He ran a hand through his hair, pacing in disbelief. "You kept this from me!"

Audra nodded. "Yes, I kept it from you. He was conceived the night of your bachelor party. You were going to marry another woman. You were on your honeymoon when I found out I was pregnant."

"I still had a right to know!" His voice rose, frustration evident. "Eight years, Audra. I missed eight years of his life!"

"I know." she said. "I know, and I hate myself for it. But I thought I was doing the right thing at the time. What newlywed man wants to find out that his yearly booty call was pregnant with his child?"

"You were not a yearly booty call," Jairo said savagely. "My feelings for you have always been complicated. I tried to stay away but couldn't. I came out here yearly for no other reason but to see you. At first, I couldn't believe you'd give me the time of day, but when you did, I was hooked." His voice was rough with emotion. "I was hooked on you, Audra. Every time I saw you, it got harder to walk away. I kept coming back because I couldn't imagine not having you in my life, even if it was just for those few stolen moments. I knew you had your plans to marry a fellow doctor and be a power couple."

He paused, then continued, "I only walked away that last time because I overheard you telling someone on the phone that you value brains over brawn and that a relationship with a dumb footballer wasn't sustainable."

Audra closed her eyes in mortification and swallowed. "I

wasn't talking about you."

Jairo's jaw tightened, his eyes flashing with frustration. "Then who were you talking about, Audra? Because it sure sounded like you were talking about me. I am a footballer."

Audra exhaled slowly, her voice soft but steady. "I was talking to Travis Pierce. We met at a frat meeting—he was on a football scholarship at university. He thought his looks meant I'd fall at his feet. I regularly insulted him every time he called me. None of my insults landed, especially that one, because he wasn't dumb—far from it. That conversation had nothing to do with you."

Jairo stared at her, his expression still hard. "You really expect me to believe that?"

"Yes, because it's the truth," Audra replied, her voice firm. "I never saw you as just a football player. You were always more than that to me. But you were getting married, and I didn't want to stand in the way of that. I thought... I thought it was best for both of us to move on."

Jairo took a step closer, his voice lowering. "But I didn't move on. I tried Audra, but no one else came close to what we had. I kept thinking about you, about the time we spent together. And now you're telling me that all this time, I had a son I didn't even know about? Do you have any idea how that feels?"

Audra's heart clenched. She reached out, but he stepped back, his emotions too intense to let her in. "I didn't know how to tell you, Jairo. I was scared you'd resent me for it, or worse, that you'd reject him. I didn't want to bring that pain into Jason's life."

"I wouldn't have rejected him," Jairo said through gritted teeth, his hands clenched at his sides. "You should've trusted me with the truth, no matter what you thought I'd do."

"I know," Audra whispered, guilt washing over her. "I was

wrong. I see that now. But I can't change the past, Jairo. All I can do is try to make things right from here."

Jairo's expression softened just a little, the anger still there but beginning to ebb. "So what now? What are we supposed to do with this?"

Audra took a deep breath, meeting his gaze with sincerity. "We co-parent, I guess. We figure out a way to raise Jason together, even if it's messy. He deserves to know you, and you deserve to know him."

Jairo ran a hand over his face, his emotions warring within him. "And us? What about us?"

"I don't know," Audra said breathlessly. "I'm at a stage where I want something more traditional than what you're offering."

Jairo nodded. "Have you given up your power couple fantasies? Because I have no intention of going to med school and becoming a doctor. I've always sucked at the sciences. I'm more of an artsy kind of guy."

Audra grimaced. "I ran out of fantasies when I had Jason. I've been dealing squarely in reality for a couple of years, and then, when I moved back home, they came back."

"No doubt fueled by your mother, who is a gigantic snob. It baffles me how she's in the helping professions and is so classist," Jairo murmured. "If it weren't for her, we would have been together by now. You know she warned me off you when I moved next door in my teens? She told me I wasn't of the right ilk. Who tells a seventeen-year-old boy that?"

"My mother, apparently," Audra sighed. "I have to go."

"Does she know I'm Jason's father?" Jairo asked.

"No," Audra opened the door. "I haven't told anyone."

"Because you were ashamed of me?" Jairo asked.

Audra paused, her hand on the doorknob, but she didn't

turn around. "It wasn't shame," she said quietly. "It was... complicated. I didn't know what to say. We were both in such different places. I was finishing med school. I was an organized, studious nerd who had it all together. Or so everyone thought. I thought it was best if a big deal wasn't made out of my pregnancy, which it would have been if they found out it was for you. You were Jairo Jones, the big football star, and married at the time. So, there was that."

Jairo inhaled. "We need to talk about that point in my life."

"I'd rather not," Audra said, glancing behind at him.

"We really need to work on communicating with each other with clothes on," Jairo said. "We excel in communicating with clothes off, but I have a feeling if we're going to make us work, we're going to need more than that."

Audra sighed. "Jairo, I'm unsure if there can be an us now."

"Why?" Jairo raised an eyebrow.

"I'll explain," Audra said. "I really do have to go."

"When can I see Jason?" Jairo asked. "I'm anxious to get to know him."

"Tomorrow," Audra said. "I'll bring him by tomorrow."

Chapter Two

After Audra left, Jairo sat in the living room and watched the lightning show beyond the patio windows. He thought back to the first time he had ever seen and interacted with Audra, their meeting again as adults, his marriage, his divorce. The memories flooded his mind—a whirlwind of emotions he had tried to suppress for years. Maybe tonight would be his one-man therapy session.

Some years ago

"Why are you staring at that girl for so long?" His mother chuckled behind him. "Go out and say hello."

"No thanks," Jairo muttered. He propped his injured leg on the chair beside him and tried to quell the sorrow he felt about being cooped up in the house because of a broken toe. All his friends were at football camp; no doubt, when his stupid toe finally healed, they would be far more advanced than he was.

He looked at the girl again—at least she offered some entertainment. His seat at the breakfast nook provided him an unfettered view of the pool area in her backyard. She was twirling and practicing cheers, a routine she had been doing for the past week. He never got tired of watching her. In his opinion, she was getting better at it.

"I wonder what her name is," he said out loud.

"I don't know her name, but I knew her mother from back in the days when we were both in high school. Back then, her name was Anastasia Parks. She was so bright. They were always making a big fuss over her brilliance." Marshalee rolled her eyes. "It got to her head. The girl was insufferable."

"Oh, really?" Jairo turned to his mother, dragging his eyes away from the girl.

"Yes," Marshalee nodded. "Couldn't stand her."

Jairo chuckled.

"And that may have something to do with my situation. I wasn't the sharpest student, and I got pregnant with your sister by your no-good father a little after fourth form and dropped out of school. But Anastasia went on to become a doctor, married another doctor, and they live up here in Park Place, Montego Bay."

Jairo chuckled. "And you live beside her. Not bad for a high school dropout."

Marshalee grinned. "And that's why I thank God every day for the lotto. It was indeed a ticket to my dreams. My only problem now is fitting in with these people. As quiet as it's kept, and as much as people like to pretend it's not a thing, classism is rife here in Jamaica. Did you know what the realtor said when I expressed an interest in this house?"

"No," Jairo said.

"He said I'd be better off in another community, that the people around here are notoriously snooty. But I will not be deterred. I will not be cowed down. I will be the classiest person on this street."

"Oh boy," Jairo muttered. "Do I have to participate?"

"No," Marshalee grinned. "You're doing enough already. You're on your way to being a famous footballer."

"With a broken toe?" Jairo grumbled.

"It will heal," Marshalee said. "And while you're down, I'm going to have to insist that you hit the books. You're a bright boy, Jairo. Football will bring you fame and money, but I want you to have options. Don't end up like me, betting on a lucky ticket to change your life. You've got potential, and you won't let it go to waste. Understand?"

Jairo sighed, glancing back out at the girl. "I hear you, Mom."

"Do you?" Marshalee crossed her arms. "I just don't want you to rely on one thing and be left with nothing if it doesn't work out. You've got more in you than just football."

Jairo knew she was right, but the frustration of being stuck at home and missing out on training, gnawed at him. He hated being sidelined, and even though he did well in school, he couldn't shake the dream of going pro. The idea of sitting behind a desk for the rest of his life just didn't appeal to him.

"Yeah, yeah," he said, turning back to the window. "I'll focus on my schoolwork. Promise."

Marshalee hugged him around the neck and kissed his forehead. "Good. I want you to be prepared for anything in this life. Devin said I should get you a tutor for the summer since CXCs are next year."

Jairo bit back a protest. If Devin said his mother should jump, she would squeal, "How high?" It was understandable.

They were indebted to Devin in so many ways. Devin had rescued them from homelessness by offering them a place to stay rent-free in one of his houses after his father had thrown them out of his place in favor of another woman and her family.

He still remembered the event in vivid detail. He was six years old—his father's sneering face, his mother's pleas. Marshalee had clutched her third child, his sister Josie, who was bawling like a banshee in her ear. Josie had been two at the time.

Marshalee had no job or place to stay, and he and his older sister, Jayla, clung together as his father had thrown out their clothes. Some of them had hit Jairo in the face.

Devin, his mother's childhood friend, had been passing by at that moment. Witnessing the commotion, he had helped them pick up their belongings from the dirt. He arranged for them to live in one of his houses, hired Marshalee to work in his shop, and helped them every step of the way.

Devin was the one who had encouraged Jairo to play football. He took him to friendly matches every Tuesday and Thursday with his buddies at the community center. It was just middle-aged men having fun, but that had shaped Jairo's love for the game.

Devin had also pulled some strings and helped Jayla get a scholarship to university. Devin was a pretty stand-up guy. He worked hard, was helpful, and had his own family. He was also a dedicated father and husband, but he always found time for their family. He was especially interested in Jairo's football career and education—he had only girls, so he lived vicariously through Jairo.

Jairo sighed. Devin's dream was for him to be a pro player but have an education with it.

He got up and hopped toward his crutches, leaning against

the settee in the family room. The one thing he didn't appreciate about this large house his mother had bought was that everything was so far away. Their previous cramped two-bedroom house could have fit in this kitchen.

"I'm going to hop outside," he yelled to his mother.

"Okay!" she yelled back.

He opened the fancy French door, crossed the patio, and gingerly descended the stairs until he came to the lawn. His mother had been talking about putting a swimming pool out here. He was indifferent.

He sat on the last step and waved to the girl. He knew she saw him—she was staring in his direction with her mouth open.

Instead of waving back like any normal neighbor, she turned her back to him and ran inside.

Maybe his mother was right, and the people at Park Place were indeed snooty.

****

It was a year later before he saw the girl up close. He had almost forgotten about her. After the day when he dared to wave at her, they moved in giant trees that blocked his view from their yard and erected a privacy screen around their pool. Just a wave had changed their landscape.

He understood it, up to a point. The world was a crazy place, and you couldn't be too careful about the people living next door. But his mother had tried to get to know the people on both sides of the fence, and her attempts to ingratiate herself with the immediate neighbors had yielded no fruit. She had even gone as far as to drag poor Josie to the Beckles Medical Center to be fitted for braces because the female Dr. Beckles was an orthodontist. The male Dr.

Beckles was a plastic surgeon.

They had been polite and courteous, but there wasn't even a hint of warmth or acknowledgment that they were neighbors.

His mother had fumed for days.

"She acted as if she was looking through me!" Marshalee had said. "And to make conversation, I mentioned that I knew her in high school and that I was Jarell's girlfriend. She glared at me as if I had stolen her man! If she had wanted him, she could've had him— that no-good, good-for-nothing, worthless piece of a man may have looked good, but he has zero value as a human being. That's why I'm raising you differently, Jairo," she ranted. "You may look like your father, but you are not going to act like him!"

Jairo had only nodded. He didn't want to be like his father either. At seventeen, with above-average looks and a local football celebrity status after being named MVP in the schoolboy football league, he was aware that he was somewhat of a girl magnet. They flocked to him like bees to honey.

He found a few of them attractive, but he wouldn't mess with his future by entertaining any of them. His father had been seventeen when he got his mother pregnant—she had been sixteen at the time. Jairo was determined to focus on football.

He had these thoughts as he walked from the neighborhood entrance to the cul-de-sac where they lived. That's where he saw her. She had one of those cutesy dogs on a leash and was strolling toward him. She was pretty up close and looked way younger than he had initially thought. How old was she? Twelve?

"Cute dog," he said casually when she came level with him.

She smiled, showing braces.

"Thanks," she said. "His name is Biscuit," she finished, glancing down at the little dog wagging its tail at Jairo. "He's kind of spoiled."

Jairo smirked, nodding as he crouched slightly to pet the dog. "Biscuit, huh? Looks more like a cupcake to me."

She giggled, and Jairo was struck by how different she was from the stuck-up girl he had assumed she would be. "I guess that's fair. He's tiny enough to be one."

Standing up, he studied her more closely. "I've seen you around," he said, gesturing toward her house. "You do those cheer routines, right? You're pretty good."

Her cheeks flushed a little, and she tucked a stray curl behind her ear. "Oh, that. Yeah, I'm on the squad at school. Just trying to get better, you know? I practice a lot."

"I could tell." Jairo chuckled, remembering all the times he'd watched her through the kitchen window. "Last year, I had a broken toe, and I was stuck at home. Watching your routines was the only fun thing I had going on for a while."

She tilted her head. "Really? I had no idea you were watching."

He turned to walk with her to the end of the road.

She glanced down at his foot as they walked. "You seem to be doing fine now. Are you back to playing?"

"Oh yes, a long time ago. I couldn't wait to get back into things." Jairo grinned. "By the way, my name is Jairo Jones. What's yours?"

"Audra Andrina Beckles," she replied with a shrug of one slim shoulder. "I wouldn't have minded if it were Andrina Audra Beckles."

Jairo chuckled. "But Audra is such a pretty name and a bit uncommon. I've never met an Audra before."

She smiled. "Really?"

"Yep," he nodded, "and I meet a lot of people."

"My dad said you're a football star," Audra said.

"He did?" Jairo raised an eyebrow. "Your folks talk about me?"

"Oh yes," Audra nodded. "Well, my dad talks about you. My mom doesn't like yours all that much. She says she's too… uh-oh." Audra stopped. "I need a cage for my mouth."

Jairo laughed. "No, go on, say whatever you want to say. I promise I won't get mad."

"I can't go on," Audra said, shaking her head. "That's house talk. House talk is house talk; what's said at home is not for road consumption."

"I get it," Jairo nodded.

"Anyway," Audra shrugged a slim shoulder, "my dad likes you. He's a fan. So does my uncle, even though he calls football 'soccer.' It's quite confusing."

Jairo laughed. "Your uncle is American, I take it? What they call football is basically a game where you barely use your feet." He grinned. "It's the weirdest thing!"

Audra giggled. "Exactly!"

They fell into a comfortable silence, walking side by side as Biscuit trotted beside them. The easy conversation felt natural as if they had known each other for longer than just a few minutes. For the first time, Jairo was glad those trees had gone up, and the privacy screen had blocked his view. It meant he had to meet Audra face to face, and that was turning out to be much better than watching her from a distance.

"So," Jairo began after a moment, "what do you want to do when you're older? Cheerleader, doctor like your mom and dad, or something else?"

Audra hesitated for a second, then answered. "I'm not sure yet. I like cheerleading, but I'm also good at science. Maybe

I'll do something different, like become a veterinarian. I love animals. My mom said she'll support whatever I do, but I should strongly consider being a people doctor and marrying one too."

What a message to tell your kid, Jairo thought, but he kept his face neutral. "So, she's got your whole life planned out, huh?"

Audra laughed softly. "Kind of, yeah. I get where she's coming from—my parents have high standards. And I'm their only child together. My dad had two children before they met, fell in love, married, and became a power couple."

"That's quite an expectation to thrust upon your young shoulders," Jairo said. "You should try to be yourself. Do something you want to do."

Audra nodded solemnly. "Of course."

Chapter Three

Jairo stirred himself from his trip down memory lane and shut off the downstairs lights. He went back to the bedroom, spread the bed with fresh sheets, and half-reclined against the headboard. He could turn on the television, but he didn't feel like it somehow. He had enjoyed the brief journey to the past.

He texted Audra: Are you home yet?

Yes, came her reply. Just had a shower. I could have stayed. Jason is firmly ensconced in bed over at my parents. It's a relief telling you about him.

Jairo still felt twinges of anger at the whole situation, but he didn't want to reopen that conversation.

Goodnight. Sleep well, he texted back.

He tossed the phone onto the bed and let his mind drift again.

Sometime in the Past

He didn't know how Devin did it, but somehow, he pulled the right strings and got Jairo a spot with one of the top football clubs in their area. It was a huge step up, and Jairo lived in St. Ann with Devin and his family for a while. Devin's wife, Cameisha, and their three daughters—twins Laura, Leah, and Reba—were part of the package. Laura and Leah were sixteen at the time, and Reba, who was Jairo's age, quickly became his friend.

Reba had a lot of issues with her super-conservative, religious mother. The two would often clash, and she'd come to Jairo for comfort, crying on his shoulder.

Jairo liked Reba, but he wasn't attracted to her. She was pretty enough, but she had no interest in enhancing her looks. Her mother had her wearing long jean skirts and sneakers, and her hair was usually kept in a messy bun. She smelled faintly of carbolic soap, the kind he associated with freshly washed clothes from his summers spent with his grandparents in Westmoreland.

Reba was the apple of Devin's eye. She was his pride and joy, his favorite girl.

"You know, Marshalee and I used to joke that our firstborns would marry one day," Devin would chuckle. "I'm making sure you have the earning power to marry Reba. She's a fine girl."

Jairo would laugh with him, though he wasn't sure how serious Devin was.

"I'm not joking," Devin would say, his tone suddenly more serious. "Tell me now—should I quit trying to make you a football star if it's all for nothing? Because the end goal, Jairo, is for you to marry Reba."

Jairo had always thought it was just another one of Devin's jokes. But as he looked into the man's eyes, something told him there was more truth to it than he expected.

"Devin, I… I don't think Reba and I are…" he began, unsure of how to continue. How could he explain that he hadn't even considered marrying Reba? Not that there was anything wrong with her, but the expectation bothered him.

"We're like family. I can't see her that way."

Devin's face tightened, though the smile never left his lips. "You've got time, Jairo. You're still young. You'll grow into it. Besides, love isn't about how you feel right now. It's about building something solid. You've got a good head on your shoulders, and Reba—well, she's going to make a fine wife one day. Mark my words."

Jairo felt the weight of Devin's words settle heavily in the pit of his stomach. He respected and admired Devin, but the idea of his future being tethered to someone simply because it was what someone else wanted didn't sit right with him. He had dreams and ambitions, and none of it included marrying a girl he didn't love.

He smiled politely and nodded, but deep down, he knew Devin's suggestion was rubbish.

"Let's focus on the football for now," Jairo had said, hoping to steer the conversation back to safe ground. "That's what I'm here for."

Devin had clapped him on the back, his smile returning to something more familiar. "Football it is, my boy. But remember, I'm thinking long-term. Just think about what I said."

He was going to community college and playing for a club he had the good fortune of leading to their first national championship. The Jamaican football league was divided into two tiers, with Jairo's club always being an underdog in the second tier.

But that year, everything changed. With Jairo as captain, they clawed their way to the finals. It was the first time in the club's history that they had even come close to a national title, and the entire community rallied behind them. The pressure was immense, but Jairo thrived under it.

On the pitch, he was a force of nature, focused and unshakable. His passion for the game fueled his every move, and soon enough, his talent caught the attention of scouts from bigger clubs in Kingston.

When his team finally lifted that trophy, Jairo stood in the center of it all, sweat dripping, heart pounding, surrounded by cheering teammates and fans. It was the moment he had dreamed of, and yet, it wasn't enough. He had worked so hard for this, but now that he had it, something still felt incomplete.

Not long after, the offers started pouring in—bigger clubs, better opportunities. Devin was thrilled; he saw it as the fulfillment of his plan, the investment in Jairo finally paying off.

But Jairo saw something else: a way out. He had no intention of staying tied to St. Ann, to Reba, or to anyone else's vision for his life. This was his moment to break free, to carve out his own path.

The night before he was set to sign with a top-tier Kingston team, Devin sat him down again.

"You've done well, Jairo. I'm proud of you. But don't forget what we discussed—your future, Reba…"

Jairo felt the knot form in his stomach again, but this time, he was ready.

"Devin," he tried to modulate his voice to be steady but firm, "I appreciate everything you've done for me. You've been like family. But I have to live my life my way. I'm not marrying Reba. I'm taking this opportunity and going after what I want."

Devin stared at him, his expression unreadable for a moment. Then, slowly, he nodded. "I see," he said quietly. "Go do what you have to do. Just don't forget where you came from and who helped you get there."

Jairo nodded. It was a veiled threat, but it didn't move him. He would never forget his roots, but there had to be a time when he could let go of the expectations placed on him. His future was in his hands now.

He played for two years in Kingston, even trained with the national team, and was placed in a few friendly matches where he got his time to shine. During that time, his mother met and married a much younger man who scammed her out of every available penny she had. It was fortunate for Jairo that she had bought the apartment in Kingston where he stayed and had given him and his sisters a hefty lump sum that she had no access to. She sold the house in Montego Bay and moved to Kingston to be with him at the townhouse, where she spent most of her days moping around, fretting about money and how much her divorce was costing her.

It was a relief when, out of the blue, he got called to play in an international match as a filler for a popular player who was out on an injury. His game was exceptional that day, and that was when he attracted the attention of scouts from a few European clubs, including one from the UK Premier League. They were impressed not only by his skill but also by his ability to adapt quickly under pressure. His phone buzzed with offers and inquiries, but the call from Brighton FC caught his attention. They wanted to fly him out for trials immediately.

His mother was ecstatic, seeing it as a chance for redemption for their family. She quickly packed up her worries and threw herself into preparing him for the journey. However, her constant fretting about money never really stopped. Despite his protests, she even borrowed money to buy him new gear for the trip. He knew, deep down, that this was more than just about him playing football—it was about giving them a fresh start.

The trials in England were grueling, but he thrived. His years of playing on uneven fields and training with limited resources had sharpened his instincts. Coaches noticed his speed, his vision, and his hunger. By the end of the week, he was offered a contract as a youth prospect with Brighton's development squad—the first step toward his Premier League dream.

And the rest was history. It was his first year on a top-tier team and he had returned to Jamaica that summer, at twenty-three. It was also a time when his family was going through significant changes. His sister, Jayla, was getting married and would move to South Africa after the wedding. She had asked him to walk her down the aisle. His mother had returned to school, earned her nursing diploma, and was working as a nurse for an elderly man who was planning to migrate to Canada and wanted her as his caretaker. His sister Josie was preparing to do her master's in the U.S. His core family was about to be scattered all over the world.

He said as much to Josie when he drove her to pick up her transcript from the university.

"I know, right?" Josie said to him. "Dad will be out here, though."

"Dad? What's a dad?" Jairo asked incredulously.

Josie looked at him sheepishly. "Our father, who art in St. Ann, Jamaica."

"The deadbeat?" Jairo snorted. "You're in touch with him?"

"Yup," Josie nodded. "When I go to St. Ann to spend time with Devin and Cameisha, I see him around. We got to talking."

"What could he say to explain his behavior toward his flesh and blood?" Jairo asked.

"He said he was under the influence of witchcraft—the lady he was with turned him against us. He said he didn't know top from bottom or right from wrong for several years."

Jairo was laughing when he stopped in front of the administration building. "Josie, you can't go to New York and be this naïve. I can't believe you fell for that made-up story."

"He's okay," Josie said stubbornly. "Once you get to know him—made up or not—he is flawed, but he is still our father. You should try to get to know him. He always talks about you and tells everybody about his football-star son. It's sickening how he has you in such high regard when I'm the one who actually speaks to him."

"Well, good for you," Jairo said. He didn't even remember what else he was going to say when exiting the admin building, he saw a grown-up Audra Beckles. He had thought about her off and on for years in an abstract way. He knew she would grow up to be a beauty, but he wasn't prepared for just how beautiful she had become. Her skin glowed with the warmth of honey, rich and golden under the sun. Her waist-length hair waved in the breeze. Her plump lips were set in a soft, unreadable expression as if she were deep in thought but aware of everything around her.

Her dark eyes, sharp and knowing, locked on him for just a second, and it felt like time had slowed down. Jairo's breath caught in his throat.

The years had done nothing to dull the connection he'd

always felt with her. If anything, it was stronger now. He watched as she crossed the courtyard, her stride graceful and confident, each step echoing with the poise of someone who had grown into herself completely.

"Jairo," his sister snapped at him impatiently. "You're acting as if you've never seen a girl. It's only Audra Beckles—we used to live beside her."

"I know," Jairo said, his voice low. "But she's a grown-up Audra Beckles. Quite, quite fine."

Josie chuckled. "You don't stand a chance with her. She has a professional bias and you're not in the right profession."

Jairo chuckled. "Does she still have that ridiculous plan to marry a doctor and be a power couple like her parents?"

"Yup," Josie nodded. "She makes it known."

"Now that's the power of parenting," Jairo murmured. "Her mother made her that way. I remember her spouting that nonsense at me when she was fourteen."

"To this day, I cannot reconcile Dr. Beckles, who is so nice and happy with me, with the harpy that Mom claims treats her like dirt and is a snob. When she was my orthodontist, she was the sweetest, kindest woman."

"She's good at her job," Jairo murmured, watching as Audra made her way toward a building labeled 'Library.' "You were her patient—how else was she supposed to act?"

Josie glared at him. "You can go and pursue Audra. I'll find my way back home. I need to check on some friends who are living on campus."

"Okay," Jairo said, dragging his eyes from Audra. "You sure?"

"Yup, my friends will take me home. And good luck pursuing Audra—you're going to need it. Neither your looks nor the fact that you're Jamaica's newest international star will do you any good with that woman. In a way, I think it will be good for you. She'll humble you."

"I am not unhumble," Jairo muttered.

Josie laughed and got out of the car. "Unhumble is not a word!"

"But it is, Miss English Major," Jairo chuckled. "Check it out."

Josie shook her head. "Don't have the time. I'll take your word for it."

Chapter Four

He watched the library entrance, contemplating going after Audra, but he didn't have to—she came out of the building and headed straight toward his car. He wound down the window and called to her as she drew level with him.

"Audra!"

She jumped and then stared at him wide-eyed. "Jairo Jones!"

"In the flesh." He smiled widely. "What are you doing this evening?"

"Studying." She moved closer to the car. "How are you doing? I haven't seen you in like five years!"

"Yep, it's been a while." Jairo flashed her a smile. "I'm out here for my sister's wedding, and then I'll take my two-month vacation out here."

Audra nodded. "That's nice. Well, have fun."

She was about to walk away—just like that? Didn't she feel the chemistry between them?

"Wait." He opened the car door and stretched a bit, hoping to show off his defined biceps. He wasn't used to a nonchalant attitude from females. He was an up-and-coming sports star; he was good-looking, and girls usually flocked to him without encouragement. And here he was, working for Audra's attention.

"Would you like to have dinner after your study session?" She hesitated.

"For old times' sake," he said quickly. "I'm more than a little curious about your life since I last saw you. I mean, you're all grown up now, and for a brief time, I considered us friends."

Audra narrowed her eyes at him. "Okay, dinner, but I'm taking my books. I have two exams left to go, and I want to ace them."

Jairo smiled. "Okay then, we can do a rain check on that date. I don't want you to mess up your exams. When you're done, we can celebrate. When is your last one?" Jairo asked, leaning forward a little, his eyes locked on hers.

Audra glanced away briefly, then back at him, her expression softening just a bit. "Next Friday. After that, I'll be free."

Jairo nodded, his smile widening. "Perfect. I'll be around. How about we celebrate then? Properly."

She smiled, though it didn't quite reach her eyes. "We'll see."

Audra pulled her bag higher onto her shoulder and gave him a slight wave before walking away.

Jairo watched her go, the feeling of unfinished business gnawing at him. Five years had passed, but there was something about her—something that intrigued him.

He sat back in his car, his mind already planning for next Friday. If it worked out, which something told him it would, he would spend all his breaks with her in Jamaica—his two months in June and July and his three weeks in December and January. He would work Audra into his schedule. He couldn't wait.

Their first date was low-key; they decided to keep things simple. Jairo had picked a quiet little restaurant tucked away from the hustle and bustle of the city. It wasn't flashy, just intimate enough for them to talk. Audra dressed in jeans and a red bandeau top to match the red headband in her hair.

She was gorgeous. He couldn't keep his eyes off her. They sat at a small table near the window, the warm lighting casting a gentle glow on her face as they talked about old times, but mostly about her studies and his career.

"So, how many girlfriends do you have?" Audra asked while they were having coffee.

Jairo chuckled. "I know this might defy belief because of my profession, but I'm not the type to sleep around."

Audra snorted.

"It's true." Jairo shrugged. "Not only am I a one-woman kind of man, I'm heavily into commitment, and I take my relationships seriously." He looked at her significantly. "I wouldn't mind if we explored a relationship."

"I don't know," Audra said. "You live in the UK; I live here. I'm going to med school; you're a footballer."

"And you haven't given up your dreams of ultimately being with a doctor," Jairo shook his head. "Tell you what, I like you, I like you a lot. I wouldn't mind if we spent the rest of the summer together."

Audra looked at him, her mouth half open.

"Stop pretending like you don't like me, too," Jairo said. "I'm not proposing marriage. I won't interfere with your plans of ultimately being with a doctor. All I'm asking is that we see where you and I go."

Audra nodded slowly. "Okay. But if we're going to do this, it has to be a secret."

"Why?" Jairo frowned.

"Because I don't want my parents to find out. I can't deal with the lectures and the general aggravation."

"Okay." Jairo nodded.

"Which means I can't tell my friends either," Audra said. "Especially my best friend, Kenny. Can you deal with that?"

"I'm not sure," Jairo said. "What if we fall in love with each other?"

"It wouldn't work anyway," Audra said. "You and I don't live in the same place, remember?"

"There is that." Jairo nodded.

"And I don't expect you to give up a lucrative career to be with me," Audra said. "Let's just focus on the here and now."

He knew that they would be singing different tunes as soon as they made love for the first time. That happened a week after their first date. After hanging out every day for a week, it became clear that they were hopelessly attracted to each other. Whatever chemicals made attraction so intense between them had taken full control.

Jairo had never felt this way before. With Audra, everything felt different—natural, yet overwhelming. He thought about her constantly, counting the hours until he could see her again. They had agreed to keep things simple, but the line between what they had and something more serious was already blurring.

He invited her to his hotel apartment a week after their first kiss. It was supposed to be just dinner, but the air between them had been electric. Before either of them realized it, they were in each other's arms, crossing a line they knew they couldn't uncross.

Afterward, lying in the dim light of her bedroom, Jairo traced circles on her bare skin, his thoughts racing. He had no idea what came next but knew one thing—this wasn't just some fleeting affair. Not for him.

"Audra," he whispered, his voice hushed, "what if we're already falling for each other?"

Audra turned her head, staring up at the ceiling. The weight of his question hung between them, heavier than either of them wanted to admit.

"Then we're in trouble," she said softly. "Because we can't afford to fall in love."

****

But he had fallen in love. Two years into their relationship, he was well and truly smitten. He tried to play it cool, though, because Audra had the uncanny knack of making him feel as if he wasn't a priority for her. What did he expect? She was hyper-focused on fulfilling a version of her life that he wouldn't factor into. It was humbling for him—he was in love with a woman who didn't prioritize him in her life, who didn't treat him special. In contrast, he was chased by others who had no qualms about stroking his ego.

After the first year, when he came to Jamaica for the summer, he told her that he didn't think it was going to work between them. His ego had been smarting.

He had booked a ticket to come back home instead of going to Canada to spend time with his mother, or to New York to spend time with Josie, or to South Africa to spend time with Jayla, who was pregnant with her first child, but Audra had been too busy for him.

She had gotten the opportunity to work at one of the most prestigious hospitals in Kingston, and her schedule had been grueling. He'd tried to be understanding, but he had only so much patience. The few times they managed to meet, she was always distracted, exhausted, or indifferent. He hated feeling like he was just another item on her endless to-do list.

She barely flinched when he told her it wouldn't work. That hurt more than anything. There was no argument, no desperate plea for him to stay—just a quiet acceptance. She'd simply nodded as if she'd been expecting it all along. "I understand," she said, her eyes void of emotion. "Maybe it's for the best."

He had left Jamaica feeling hollow. He had wanted her to fight for him, to show some sign that he mattered to her. But she didn't. He was just one more thing she could let go of, and that was a harsh reality he wasn't prepared for.

Yet despite everything, he couldn't shake her from his mind. Audra had this magnetic pull over him. Even when she wasn't around, he found himself thinking about her, replaying their conversations, wondering what she was doing. His heart had a mind of its own, and even though his brain told him to move on, his heart was stubborn.

Two months after that breakup, she called him out of the blue, just as he started to find peace. Her voice was tired, but there was something different—vulnerability, maybe. She didn't apologize, but she didn't have to. The fact that she called at all was enough to reel him back in.

"I miss you," she'd whispered over the line, and suddenly, nothing else mattered.

That's how their on-again, off-again saga had begun.

He met her in New York that Christmas, and they lived together for five weeks. They were hungry for each other, as they always were. He actually thought it was a sign that they had something workable.

But alas, he heard her over the phone that summer, the day before he left, mentioning to someone that she appreciated brains over brawn and wouldn't be messing with a footballer. It had hurt. It had cut deep. He didn't even tell her that he had overheard her conversation. He had ended it. He had vowed to forget her this time, but his heart wouldn't let him. No matter how hard he tried to move on, Audra was always there, lingering in the back of his mind like a song he couldn't shake. He'd buried himself in his career and dated other women, but none made him feel like she did.

Her words haunted him—she appreciated 'brains over brawn'. Was that really how she saw him? Just another athlete without substance? He had tried to brush it off, but the sting of her casual dismissal gnawed at him. It wasn't just the insult but the realization that she had never truly seen him. Despite all their time together, all their late-night conversations, and shared dreams, she still saw him as something he wasn't.

It wasn't until a year later, when he was at the height of his career that she reappeared in his life. When she called, he had just signed the biggest contract of his career, his face plastered all over the news. It was just like Audra to pop back in when he least expected it.

"I've been thinking about you," she said softly, as if nothing had changed between them.

And just like that, the cycle started again. He let her back in, against his better judgment, because no matter how much pain she caused him, he couldn't let her go. She was his addiction, and he was helpless against the pull. Every time they were together, it felt like they were on the cusp of something great, but every time it fell apart, it left him more broken than before.

He probably would have still been on the Audra Beckles

roller coaster if his mother hadn't called him, sobbing, "Devin is dying, and he is asking for you."

He was shocked. After getting his mother to calm down, she sobbed out the story. Devin's mentally ill older brother, who had been incarcerated, had been released from prison and had staked a claim on all the property that Devin owned because it had been inherited from their deceased parents.

Devin had fought the preposterous claim because he had grown the business far past what his parents had left and added a few properties to their rental portfolio over the years. But his brother didn't see it that way, and they battled it out in court. Before the case could go anywhere, Devin's brother, in a fit of madness, had burned down the family house. Devin, his wife Cameisha, and the twins, Laura and Leah, had been at home.

Reba had gone to a church retreat. That was the only thing that saved her. Cameisha and the twins were not so lucky.

Devin did not die immediately; he was badly burned and hanging on for dear life when Jairo went to visit him in the hospital. He was in a state but still coherent. "Promise me you'll take care of Reba."

"I promise," Jairo had said solemnly.

"Marry her and take her away from here," Devin had clutched his arm. "She has no one left. Just you."

Jairo opened his mouth to protest, but when he remembered all the things Devin had done for him and the fact that he was a little heart-sore about Audra, he nodded, even though his heart was racing. He had no idea what he was agreeing to, but in that moment, looking at Devin's broken body and knowing the weight of his friend's loss, he couldn't say no. Devin had been like a father to him, and now he was asking for the one thing Jairo never thought he'd be responsible for—marrying Reba.

"I'll take care of her; I'll marry her," Jairo had promised, his voice thick with emotion. Devin's grip loosened as if those words had given him peace. But the weight of the promise pressed down on Jairo like a leaden chain.

Marrying Reba was never part of his plan, and the idea of doing it out of obligation made his chest tighten. But how could he refuse a dying man? Especially when Devin had done so much for him over the years?

As he left the hospital that day, Jairo was torn. His thoughts drifted back to Audra, the woman he could never forget. Despite their relationship being a roller coaster of pain and passion, he still loved her.

But Audra was complicated and elusive, and she slipped away every time he tried to hold on to her. On the other hand, Reba was stable, kind, and, most importantly, she needed him.

Jairo spent the next few weeks wrestling with the decision. Reba, devastated by the loss of her mother and sisters, had retreated into herself. She was alone, grieving, and Jairo was the only one left to offer her comfort. He felt a growing sense of responsibility toward her, and part of him wondered if this was his chance to start fresh. Maybe he could build something different, something steady, with Reba.

His mother was the one who convinced him to do it.

"Marry her, move her to Kingston, or take her out of the country. Devin's brother is still at large," Marshalee had urged him. "He could come back and hurt her."

And so he had done it. It was supposed to be a low-key wedding, but one of his friends, Noah Honeyghan, had gotten wind of it, broadcasted it to the news, and convinced him to have a bachelor party.

That was when Audra came back into his life. She had shown up at the hotel he always stayed, and seeing her again was like a sledgehammer to his system. The timing was impeccable, almost cruel.

Suddenly, Jairo was pulled back into the emotional tug-of-war between the woman he couldn't let go of and the woman he had promised to care for. Every time he thought he had moved on from Audra, she reappeared, reminding him of the life they might have had. But with Reba's future hanging in the balance, Jairo knew he had a choice to make.

Keep chasing a dream that might never come true, or honor the promise he made to his dying friend? On his way from his bachelor party, he had stared at Audra in the hotel lobby and had told himself just one more night with her. That was all. Then he wouldn't come back to Jamaica. He wouldn't seek out her social media, he would lose her number, and he would cut her off cold turkey.

In order to have a successful marriage with Reba, he had to do it. Little did he know that he would impregnate her that night. And now, here he was—an absentee father, just like his dad had been to him.

He pulled the pillow over his face. Finding out he was a father was just sinking in; he was overwhelmed by the weight of it all. The realization that he was repeating his father's mistakes tore at him. He had vowed never to be like his dad—absent, detached, more concerned with his own life than his responsibilities. But here he was, miles away from the son he didn't even know existed until a few hours ago.

Jason. His son.

Jairo couldn't even wrap his mind around it. Audra had hidden this from him for eight years. He didn't know if he was more furious or heartbroken. All those times he had come back to Jamaica, all those near-misses where their lives could've intertwined again, she had kept him in the dark. She had robbed him of being there from the start—those first steps, first words, the precious moments every father dreamed of.

But could he really blame her? After all, he had cut her off. In those days, there was no way she could have gotten in touch with him. He would have resisted. The guilt gnawed at him. He wasn't just an absentee father; he had been absent from his own life, living in a constant state of half-commitment. Torn between his obligations to Reba and the love he couldn't let go of for Audra, Jairo had been stuck in limbo for years.

Now, it was time to face reality. Audra wasn't just a memory or a mistake from his past. She was the mother of his child. And Jason, innocent in all this, deserved better than what Jairo had given so far. He couldn't run from this. He had to figure out how to be a father, how to build something real with Audra if that was even possible, or at least figure out how to co-parent.

He tossed the pillow aside and sat up, running his hands over his face. His life was a mess, but it was his mess to clean up. One way or another, he would have to make things right—with Audra and, most importantly, Jason. There was no more running, no more excuses.

Chapter Five

"It's awfully quiet in here. Good morning, darling!" Anastasia said, striding into the breakfast area. She was dressed impeccably, in her black pencil skirt, white silk blouse, and her ever-present pearls. Her hair was freshly blow-dried and hung to her mid-back in a smooth waterfall. Anastasia was still unmistakably pretty. It was as if she was aging like fine wine. Her mother's medium brown skin was wrinkle-free and smooth, like a woman in her twenties or thirties. And she barely wore makeup.

Audra looked at her mother enviously. She was so self-assured and confident in her skin. When would she be like that? Was this self-assuredness something that she would ever develop, or would she be doomed to faking it like she had been doing?

She had stayed up last night, tossing and turning, thinking about what a mess she had made of her life. She had been thinking about Jairo, his proposal for them to have a more serious relationship, and the fact that she had finally told him about Jason. She was still conflicted about that. She didn't know why she had said anything. She had gone to his house after getting a text and directions to the place he was staying, and that was as far as she had planned to go with the conversation. She hadn't intended to drop the bombshell about Jason, but it had slipped out in the heat of the moment, and now everything was more complicated.

"Audra!" Her mother sat before her after pouring out coffee. "It is polite to respond 'good morning' when someone says it."

Audra nodded. "So sorry, I was lost in thought."

"And you look like you didn't get enough sleep," Anastasia said. "You shouldn't look so ragged if you are going to see patients, darling. They expect their doctors to be the picture of health. It gives them something to aspire to."

"True," Audra murmured. She expected she did look a little ragged, but when had her mother ever not had a complaint about her looks? At this very table, for most of her life, it was always something: "You are too fat, too skinny, too short, too tall. Your hair is too lank, too shiny, too curly, too straight. Your teeth are too crooked, too straight, too yellow, too white." There was always something.

It's a wonder she had grown up relatively okay. The chip on her shoulder should have been bigger than it was, and her insecurities more than a mile wide. But then again, she had her dad, who usually mitigated the worst criticisms with his effusive praise.

And he was a plastic surgeon, so his words had more weight. Besides, she looked a lot like her mom, just a lighter version of her. There had to be some psychological reason why her mother kept criticizing her.

She distracted herself by trying to remember the term.

What was it again? Projection, that was it. Her mother was projecting her own insecurities onto her. She was also a manipulator, trying to turn Audra into Anastasia 2.0: Marry a doctor, Audra. Return to Jamaica and start practicing. Eventually, you'll be running the family practice with your doctor spouse. That is exactly how it should be.

"Are you even listening, Audra?" Her mother's sharp tone cut through her thoughts.

"Yes, Mom. I heard you." Audra took a deep breath and forced a smile. "I'll make sure I look more presentable before heading to the medical center."

Her mother sighed, shaking her head slightly. "It's not just about appearances, darling. It's about discipline and setting standards for yourself. It's about being... more."

More. Always more. It was exhausting.

"Our newest doctor on staff, Douglas Mitchell, has been popping in and out of the building."

"Didn't notice," Audra said.

"He is in your department," Anastasia said. "He asked about you. Apparently, he saw you in the lobby area yesterday. He was quite interested in you after seeing you."

"Is that so?" Audra looked at her mother with interest.

"I can't believe you haven't seen him around," Anastasia said. "We recruited him weeks ago. He needed to tie up some loose ends from his old workplace, but he's been popping in and out. He's all anyone else is talking about. He's forty, handsome, divorced, and single."

"Yay for him," Audra said.

"I was thinking, yay for you," her mother chuckled. "He has the cutest English accent. His mother is Nigerian, and his father is British. They're both medical doctors."

"Wow, sounds like male Audra," Audra said snarkily.

Anastasia glared at her. "Except he doesn't have a child

out of wedlock with an unknown woman."

"Give it a break," Audra sighed.

"It's preposterous that I do not know my grandson's father," Anastasia said. "Why can't you tell me who it is?"

"Because I don't want to," Audra said.

"Good morning, everyone," Mabel entered the kitchen. "You're both up early."

Audra exhaled. Mabel was their housekeeper—her mother's cousin, actually. She had fallen on hard times several years ago, and Anastasia had hired her to help out their main housekeeper. Their main housekeeper, Sidney, had migrated, and since then, Mabel had taken over full-time. She was usually overly familiar with Anastasia, which got under her skin, and she refused to wear a uniform like the other housekeepers around the neighborhood. But apart from that, she ran the house with a shrewd efficiency. And best of all, she was trustworthy and honest.

Mabel was the only reason Audra knew certain things about her mother's history.

"I am so glad to see you," Audra said to Mabel. "My mother was once more harassing me about the identity of Jason's father."

"You should be used to that by now," Mabel chuckled. "Let me go and get Jason ready for school. Do you guys need anything special for breakfast?"

"Nothing for me, please," Anastasia said. "I'll be attending a midmorning brunch at a medical conference. I'll top up then."

"Eggs and toast for Jason, I'll just have fruits," Audra said. "And thanks, Mabel, for looking out for him last night."

"No problem, he's no bother at all," Mabel said. "He just needs his iPad and fantasy football game, and it's as if I was alone."

"That's not healthy," Anastasia murmured. "I should find out if there are any good science games for him to play."

"Good luck with that," Mabel snorted. "He's obsessed with the football one. He has his favorite virtual players and gets really into it. I tried suggesting other games, but once he's hooked, there's no turning back." Mabel shook her head and smiled.

"Well, maybe I'll ask him later," Anastasia said, with that thoughtful expression Audra had come to expect whenever her mother turned her critical eye to someone's development. "He might surprise you."

Audra sighed. "Let him be a kid, Mom. He's just eight."

Anastasia raised an eyebrow. "That's precisely why setting proper habits now is important, Audra. If you don't instill discipline in him at this age, what happens when he's older? You don't want him to end up choosing sports over science as a career, do you? When you were eight, I had you doing the high school biology syllabus."

Audra rubbed her temples, feeling a headache forming. The ongoing tug-of-war between what her mother thought was best and what Audra believed Jason needed was exhausting. She had only been in Jamaica for four months. Was this the way her life was going to be?

Moving away from her parents' house was looking more and more attractive. Unfortunately, there were benefits to staying here in the short term. She tallied the benefits in her head: free accommodation in their guest house, a nice neighborhood, close proximity to Jason's school, and twenty-four-seven babysitting services from Mabel, who lived in a suite downstairs and had no personal life at the moment. Mabel didn't mind babysitting one bit; she even gladly did the drop-offs and pick-ups when Audra got tied up at work.

"Back to Douglas Mitchell," her mother said, intruding on her thoughts. "I was thinking he would make the perfect partner for you. Our lives would mirror each other somewhat."

"How?" Audra asked.

"Well, not exactly alike, obviously," Anastasia said. "After all, you are a single mother, but he is divorced with two children, just like your father was when I met him. He was like a rudderless ship, waiting for the right woman to steer him into peaceful waters."

Audra chuckled. "I really don't want stepchildren at the moment. I can barely manage my own child."

Anastasia nodded. "That's the thing. Their mother doesn't live here. Like me, you'd only need to see your stepchildren on the holidays. And, as you know, I got on splendidly with your brother and sister."

Audra snorted. "Malia and Kirk were afraid of you when they were younger."

"I doubt that," Anastasia said dismissively. "They were just introverts. I brought them out of their shell."

"You mean you forced them out of their shell because they were so intimidated by you," Audra said. "You enjoy being intimidating."

"Well, a little intimidation never hurt," Anastasia replied smoothly. "It's a useful tool. Keeps people in line, and it worked wonders with you and your siblings. All of you did well in life. When Malia got her doctorate in anthropology, who was the first one she called?"

"You," Audra sighed. It was baffling how her sister was closer to Anastasia than her parents. Maybe because Malia was never under pressure to become a medical doctor and marry one. Anastasia had never required her stepchildren to follow in her footsteps. She treated them with a warm friendship devoid of heavy expectations. They could be themselves, forge their paths, and marry who they wanted. Malia was five years older than Audra and had recently gotten married to a fellow anthropologist— a heavily tattooed fruitarian who lived in the mountains of Colorado. Her parents had flown out for the wedding.

Anastasia had even gone as far as to wear one of Malia's organic cotton dresses and a flower crown for the occasion.

If it had been her wedding, Audra had a feeling Anastasia would not have attended, much less worn that outfit.

Not to mention Kirk— he was an engineer but had three children out of wedlock, the last one with a girl here in Jamaica. The child was two years old now.

What did Anastasia do when she heard? She offered her congratulations to her stepson. Not one word was mentioned about marriage, what profession the mother had, or why Kirk didn't take any relationship seriously. Nope. All of that was reserved for her.

Thankfully, her mother took a phone call, leaving her to think in peace. A few minutes later, Jason bounded into the kitchen in his khaki suit, looking like a mini Jairo Jones. The older he got, the more he resembled his father. He just had her lighter complexion and silkier hair. Other than that, he was all Jairo.

She sighed. It hadn't occurred to her until this year how much he was growing to look like his father. He was tall for his age, and they even had the same whisky-colored eyes.

"Morning, Mom! Hi, Nana!"

Anastasia blew him a kiss.

Jason glanced at Mabel with a wide grin. "Thanks for letting me stay up a little late last night."

"You're welcome, kiddo. Just don't tell your mom," Mabel winked.

Audra smiled despite herself. "Don't make it a habit."
Jason sat down and immediately took out his iPad.
"You and that thing," Audra muttered.
"I have time," Jason glanced at the clock. "Can I play one game? I promise to eat all my breakfast."
"Okay," Audra nodded.
Audra watched him fondly as he stared at the screen in concentration. He was oblivious to the fact that she had told his father about him. And now, she would have to tell him about his father. She had already told Jason his father wasn't in his life and didn't know about him. So, this revelation would surprise her son—a happy surprise, she hoped.
It had been just the two of them for the last couple of years. She would have to find some time today to talk to him. Maybe when she was taking him to school.
Her father came into the kitchen dressed semi-casually. He greeted them politely, kissed her forehead, and sat at the breakfast nook.
"What would you like to eat, Samuel?" Mabel asked.
"Anything Jason is having," Samuel replied, picking up the morning paper. "I trust his palette."
Audra grinned. Her father was the fun dad. He was laid-back by nature; he didn't let anything bother him. He was playful, friendly, and more likely to joke about something than be serious.
His personality meant that Anastasia had to take on a more serious role in their relationship, and she was unmistakably the leader. Everyone knew that—Samuel knew it and celebrated it. Anastasia was the wheel that kept him turning. She was the organizer. When she was around, the business and household ran smoothly.
Audra had inherited that trait from her mother, as well as other traits she had to grudgingly admit. She was anal, an

organizer, and tended to come off as bossy.

Audra looked between the two of them. They made for a striking couple—they were both in their late fifties and early sixties but still looked youthful. They took care of themselves, still obviously loved each other, still had date nights, went away on cruises, and finished each other's sentences. They weren't perfect, but they worked. How could she have had such an example and done so poorly at relationships?

Not relationships—her one relationship.

Mabel served breakfast. Audra ate her fruit while her mother came off the phone and started a discussion about a friend's daughter who had found out she was pregnant and had the audacity not to tell her parents who the father was. Her friend called her to commiserate because she had gone through the same thing with Audra.

"This generation of women..." her mother huffed, glaring at Audra. "So secretive, so independent. You all think you can just handle everything on your own, without guidance, without family. And when we give our input, we're shunned, pushed aside, and told to keep quiet."

Her father lowered his paper. "Ana, let it go."

He glanced at his watch. "Don't you have an early conference?"

"I do," Anastasia huffed. She got up, kissed her husband, and glared at Audra. "Have a good day, everyone."

Audra exhaled when her mother left the kitchen. "You do realize I go through this every single day, don't you? Sometimes I wonder why I came back home for this."

"You two," Samuel said, "are so incredibly stubborn. You refuse to tell her, and she refuses to stop asking."

Audra glanced at Jason. Thankfully, he was not even remotely interested in their conversation—he was shoveling eggs into his mouth and glancing at his screen.

"I am going to tell him today," Audra said out loud. "After that, I'll tell Mom. I'm just going to have to work myself up to it."

"Good," her father nodded. "That will hopefully lead to peace between you and Ana."

"Why haven't you ever been as curious as Mom?" Audra frowned. "I don't get it."

"Because I'm a football fan, remember?" her father said. "I watched a certain former footballer give a retirement interview, and it didn't take a genius to figure it out after that. The boy looks like his father. I figured you two met while you were at university, and he visited Kingston. You connected over him, having lived next door when you were younger."

"You are spot on," Audra gasped. "You knew, and you didn't tell Mom?"

Her father grinned. "It's not my news to tell."

Chapter Six

"**S**o, Jason," Audra said as they were on their way to school, "remember how I told you that I didn't tell your dad about you because of the circumstances leading up to your birth?"

Jason looked over at her with eyes so much like Jairo's. "Yes."

"Well, I found your dad, and he wants to meet you," Audra said. "Today, after school, we'll go to his place."

Jason's eyes widened, and he sat up straighter in his seat. "Really? You're not joking, right?"

Audra smiled softly. "I wouldn't joke about this, baby. I know it's a lot to take in, but your dad is excited to see you. He's been waiting for this for a long time."

Jason was quiet for a moment, biting his lip as he stared out the window. "What if he doesn't like me?"

Audra's heart squeezed at the vulnerability in his voice. "Oh, honey, your dad is going to love you. There's no way he wouldn't. You're smart, funny, and kind. He's going to be so proud of you."

Jason glanced at her, still uncertain. "Are you sure?"

"I'm positive," Audra said, reaching over to squeeze his hand. "And I'll be right there with you. We're in this together, okay?"

Jason nodded slowly, but the hint of a smile tugged at the corner of his lips. "Okay."

She dropped him off at the designated place. It was a small prep school, fancier than the one where she had gone, and it cost an arm and a leg. But it came highly recommended by her cousins, and she had reasoned that at least Jason would have people he knew there.

Jason was bristling with excitement when he left the car. His teacher, Miss Henry, stopped her before she could drive away. It seemed as if she was just coming in to work.

"Dr. Beckles," Miss Henry said, "you didn't respond to my email about extracurricular activities."

"I didn't?" Audra tried to wrack her brain, searching for a missed email in her mind's eye. She was coming up blank.

"At our school, we have extracurriculars for our students. We usually ask parents to get involved; it helps build a sense of community and gives the students even more support," Miss Henry explained. "We understand how busy parents can be, but any involvement, even just attending a few events or helping organize a fundraiser, goes a long way. Jason signed up for football and swimming, and we always like to see parents cheering from the sidelines or assisting where they can."

Audra nodded, her mind racing. The last thing she had time for was volunteering at school events, especially with her new job at the practice. But she didn't want Jason to feel like he was missing out or that she wasn't invested in his interests.

"I really appreciate you letting me know," Audra said carefully. "I'll see what I can do. Jason loves both sports, so I'll see how involved I can be."

"Maybe his father can lend a hand?" Miss Henry suggested. "We would welcome a parent coach in the football area."

Audra froze. "I'll… I'll ask him."

"Great!" Miss Henry smiled. "Could we get his email to add to the parent roster?"

"Sure," Audra said, "I'll text it to you."

What had she agreed to? She wondered as she drove away. And why, today of all days, did Miss Henry have to ask about Jason's father? Why had she volunteered poor Jairo? He had yet to meet Jason, and she didn't know if he was good with kids. He had just found out he had a son, and now she was volunteering him to coach twenty more.

Maybe it wasn't such a bad idea, she tried to reassure herself. Jairo and Jason could bond over football.

They would start with something familiar—sports, which she knew he was passionate about.

But still, coaching a whole team?

Her phone rang. It was her bestie, Kenny. Audra answered.

"Hey, Miss Newly Engaged. What's going on?"

Kenny squealed. "I am so excited! Camden and I set a wedding date this morning!"

"Cool," Audra said. "When are you thinking?"

"Boxing Day. We're still brainstorming about the venue."

"Wow, sounds good," Audra said. "But Boxing Day is four months away. That's short notice."

Kenny laughed. "I thought it was too long. Camden and I wanted to ditch the wedding hullabaloo, but our mothers said no. I'm having a brainstorming session next weekend with my girls to agree on a place to host my wedding. I'll have it catered. Come by at three."

"Sure," Audra said, "looking forward to it."

"Great," Kenny said, and hung up.

She didn't even get to tell Kenny about the latest happenings in her life. And she probably wouldn't. Kenny was excited, and she didn't want to bring her troubles to the fore and be a wet blanket.

She drove up to Beckles Medical Center, a sprawling complex with more than twelve specialties. Her parents had built the practice from the ground up; it was Jamaica's largest physician-owned group practice. They had a production-based profit model, where each doctor earned a share of the revenue based on the number of patients they treated and procedures they performed. It fostered competition, which her parents saw as healthy, but Audra knew it also created tension among the doctors. Still, the model had made the practice incredibly successful, attracting top talent nationwide.

They had built a new pediatric wing just because she had chosen that to be her specialty. She knew that decision was driven by her mother, even though major decisions, such as adding a pediatric wing to the complex, were made collectively, often requiring a unanimous vote. It was a lot of pressure to have a whole building prepared for her to start working. Of course, she could have said no and refused to come home and practice, but her mother had been prepping her for this since childhood. It took a lot of work to go against the programming. Besides, this wasn't just a workplace. It was the embodiment of her parents' expectations—a reminder of the life she was meant to have.

She was supposed to marry a doctor, and together they would take over when her parents retired. She stepped inside the lobby area and was greeted by the sweet smell of basil and spearmint. Her mother believed that a medical center should smell like a spa. This was Audra's favorite combination of the scents they had in rotation.

She was standing in the lobby, sniffing the air—inhale, exhale—letting the scent wash over her. Basil was supposed to be good for stress and focus. She needed every bit of that today. Audra allowed herself a brief moment of calm as the soothing aroma filled her senses. The past few days had been chaotic but this familiar scent grounded her, if only for a moment.

"You know, I find myself doing the very same thing," a voice said behind her.

Audra spun around. A tall, dark, handsome, muscular guy dressed semi-casually, with a doctor's jacket hooked over his shoulder, looked at her and smiled slowly. A dimple appeared on his cheek.

"Hello, I'm Douglas Mitchell. The newest kid on the block. Pediatric surgery is my specialty."

"Oh, yes," Audra nodded. "I heard about you."

"I hope it's all good things," Douglas said, his smile widening as he extended his hand. "I've heard great things about you, too, Dr. Beckles. It's nice to finally meet you in person."

Audra took his hand, feeling a spark of warmth in his grip. "Nice to meet you, too. My mom told me this morning that you would be joining us in pediatrics. Welcome to Beckles Medical Center."

"Thanks! I'm excited to be here. This place has such a great reputation, and when I heard there was a pediatric section, I immediately applied," he said, his enthusiasm evident. "I'm really looking forward to contributing."

She smiled, feeling a flicker of camaraderie. "We have a great team. You'll fit right in. When do you officially start?"

"Next week," he smiled. "I'm still in the process of sorting out my living situation and getting settled. But I've been moving into my office steadily over the past week and getting acquainted with the place."

Audra nodded. "I know how that feels. I moved back to Jamaica four months ago with my son and settling in took me a while."

"Oh, you have a son?" he smiled. "How old is he?"

"Eight," Audra said. "Just dropped him off at school. At least he likes his new school. I was anxious about that for a while."

"I probably would be, too, if I had the kids with me," Douglas said. "But they're with my ex-wife in Barbados. She has to deal with the hassle of getting them settled and sorted."

"Oh…" Audra was curious about his situation and wanted to ask more questions, but they had just met. No doubt, they would have time to talk some more.

"Dr. Beckles, Dr. Mitchell," Arlene, the practice manager, greeted them warmly. "How are you both?"

"Good," Audra murmured.

Douglas smiled. "Great."

"Dr. Beckles, please check your email and get back to us about the staff meeting tomorrow? We need to know if you'll be there," Arlene said.

She chatted with them a bit and then left.

"I'm going to have to check that email," Audra murmured. "This is the second time I've missed out on mail. Apparently, I need to check it every day. I'll see you around, Dr. Mitchell."

"Please, call me Douglas," Douglas said, "or Mitchell."

Audra smiled. "Well, call me Audra then. And have a good day."

Chapter Seven

"**I** am bringing Jason to meet you at five," Jairo read the text. His interior decorator was showing him around, and he tuned her out for a moment. She knew her job really well. He hadn't expected anything less—she came highly recommended by Richard Tinsdale, his friend from college and the property developer.

They had already done an online consultation, and though he was a bit taken aback by the youthfulness and beauty of Kendrea Carter, after seeing her professionalism, he was confident enough to let her speak while his mind wandered.

He was going to meet his son today. His breath hitched as the weight of that realization settled in. Jason. His son. Jairo hadn't been able to stop thinking about him since Audra had dropped the bombshell last night. At the time, he wasn't sure what to feel—shock, guilt, maybe a little anger at having missed so much—but now, anticipation gnawed at him.

He glanced up, realizing the decorator was waiting for

his input. "Uh, yeah, that looks fine," he muttered, his eyes drifting back to his phone. Five o'clock. Just a few hours away.

Could he do this? Would Jason even like him?

His heart raced. This was different from closing deals or navigating boardrooms. This was fatherhood. The very thing he'd once thought he might never get a chance at while married to Reba.

"That's the wrong response," Kendrea said, breaking his thoughts. "I asked you if leather or cloth settees would be appropriate for the family room."

"Oh, sorry," Jairo said sheepishly. "What would you recommend? I have a son. I anticipate he will come over a lot or maybe even live here with me eventually."

Kendrea's eyebrows shot up in surprise, and she seemed momentarily at a loss for words. "Oh! Congratulations! That's wonderful news! I'd recommend cloth settees for a family-friendly environment—more comfortable and easier to clean, especially with kids around."

Jairo nodded, though his mind was still whirling. "Right, cloth it is," he said absently, his thoughts drifting back to Jason. What would he be like? What was he like at eight years old?

He should ask Audra for a picture. The thought of his son in this space, laughing and playing, made the house feel suddenly alive.

"Is everything okay?" Kendrea asked, tilting her head as she studied him.

"Yeah, just… a lot on my mind." He ran a hand through his hair, trying to shake off the anxiety. "I'm meeting him for the first time today."

She smiled gently. "That's a big moment. Just be yourself. Kids can sense when someone is being genuine."

He appreciated the encouragement, but the thought of his son's reaction made his stomach churn. What if Jason didn't want to be around him? What if he thought he was just another stranger?

As Kendrea moved on to discuss paint colors and the slight changes she had made, Jairo found it hard to focus. He needed to make this right.

"So, how long will this take?" Jairo asked.

"Two months," Kendrea replied. "We have to order some of the pieces. It could be a month, but I like to give myself some wiggle room."

"Can we say six weeks?" Jairo murmured. "I'll have a grand housewarming party then. I can introduce my son to my family and friends in one go."

"The downstairs patio with the infinity pool is a nice place to throw a party," Kendrea nodded. "I often wonder why my sister doesn't utilize hers more. It's the perfect setup. There's that gorgeous sea view; you could set up tables, chairs, and food stations. I know of a friend who can do the catering. She deals with affluent clients like yourself all the time."

"Your sister lives over here?" Jairo asked curiously.

"Yes," Kendrea nodded. "Her name is Kenny Carter. She lives with Camden Byfield right next door."

Jairo chuckled. "Someone once told me that Jamaica is like a small town, and we have three degrees of separation between us if that. I scoffed at them then. I'm now on my way to being convinced."

Kendrea looked at him curiously. "What are you talking about?"

"Your sister is Audra's best friend."

"Yup," Kendrea nodded. "Two peas in a pod, those two."

Jairo smiled. "I see. It may not be so hard to convince Audra to move in with me then, with her best friend next door."

Kendrea gasped and then laughed. "Oh my, I was wondering why you looked so familiar. I mean, apart from the fact that I've seen you on TV. Jason is the spitting image of you."

"You know Jason?" Jairo asked.

"I do, quite well. In the past, I used to babysit for Audra when she came out for vacations. It was the best summer job," Kendrea said fondly. "It didn't feel like work, and she paid well."

Jairo smiled. "I want them both in my life."

"Tell you what," Kendrea said briskly, "if you want Audra to move in, let her help with the decoration process. Run your plans by her, ask her opinion on things. I initially thought this would have been a bachelor pad, but it seems you want to live with your family. Audra's picky. You don't want to have to redo your décor twice."

Jairo nodded. "That's right."

"Well, having Audra's opinion will be a good thing, especially if she's going to live here too," Kendrea said. "Let me know if you'd like me to consult with the two of you on this."

Jairo smiled. "Thank you, that's a great suggestion, Kendrea."

"If you want to have your party in six weeks, you've got to work with alacrity," Kendrea said. "I'll send our agreed-upon adjustments this evening, and then you can show them to Audra."

Jairo followed Kendrea out and got into his car. The building had a state-of-the-art security system—he didn't even have to lock up. He liked it here; it felt right. He could see himself living with Audra, Jason, and their other children.

He called his lawyer before driving out. He needed to make Jason his beneficiary and legally acknowledge him.

It would be a challenging conversation because his lawyer was also his ex-wife.

"Reba Jones," she answered the phone briskly.

Jairo chuckled. "You sound a tad bit irritated."

"Jairo!" Reba chuckled. "I was irritated with someone else, not you, never you. How are you?"

"Good," Jairo said. "I found out yesterday that I have a son. I need to know the process to make him my beneficiary."

Reba gasped. "Say what?"

Jairo chuckled. "You heard."

"Are you pleased about it?" Reba asked.

"Yes," Jairo said. "Quite so. He's eight years old. Conceived on the night of my bachelor party. His mother didn't tell me because I was married to you at the time."

"Oh no," Reba murmured. "She should have said something. Eight years old, wow. Is he here in Jamaica or…?"

"He is here," Jairo said.

"Are you sure he's yours?" Reba asked.

"Apparently, we look alike. I haven't met him yet," Jairo said.

"Hold up," Reba chuckled. "I'm going to close my office door. I'm about to ask you a lot of questions."

Jairo laughed. "Ask away."

"So, who is this woman?"

"Audra Beckles," Jairo said promptly.

"Oh," Reba gasped. "Audra, the woman who broke your heart, who thought you weren't good enough for her. I don't like her."

"I know," Jairo said, "but I do, and I really want to have a relationship with her."

"Uh huh," Reba snorted.

"So, as my lawyer, what's your opinion about this situation?"

"We do a DNA test," Reba said, speaking in her professional voice. "And then we go through the legal process to amend your will and any insurance policies you may have. Once we establish paternity, we can set things in motion. It's a fairly straightforward process, but emotionally… that's another story."

Jairo exhaled, feeling the weight of the situation settle in. "Yeah, the emotions are all over the place."

"I bet," Reba said, sympathy creeping into her voice. "You know this is a huge step, right? Adding a child to your life is one thing, but if you're considering rekindling something with Audra…"

"I know," Jairo said. "But she is the one. She's always been the one. I've never managed to shake her out of my system, and I probably never will."

Reba sighed. "Well, for what it's worth, Jairo, I hope it works out. Just… be careful. And ensure you're not getting your heart broken again."

"Thanks," he said quietly. "I appreciate that."

"Alright then," Reba said, her professional tone returning. "I'll start drawing up the paperwork for the DNA test. Once that's confirmed, we can move forward with everything else. Keep me posted."

"I will," Jairo replied. "And Reba… thanks."

"It's not a problem at all," she said softly before ending the call.

Jairo sat in his car for a moment, processing everything. Audra, Jason, Reba... his entire world was changing, and he needed to be ready for whatever came next.

Chapter Eight

Five o'clock couldn't come fast enough for Jairo. He restlessly paced the floors of his luxurious rental house until he saw Audra's car on the camera at the gate.

And then he became nervous. This was the most nervous he had ever been, and he had gone through his fair share of nerves, especially before playing a big game.

He wiped his palms on his jeans and took a deep breath, feeling the weight of what was about to happen. It wasn't just seeing Audra again—it was meeting his son for the first time—the son he didn't even know he had. His heart raced as he heard the soft hum of the gate opening.

A few moments later, there was a knock on the door. Jairo hesitated for a split second, then walked over and opened it.

Audra stood there, looking as composed as ever, though her eyes betrayed a mix of anxiety and anticipation. Beside her stood Jason, holding onto her hand, wide-eyed and curious. Jairo's breath caught in his throat as he took in the boy standing before him—tall for his age, with curly hair and light brown eyes that mirrored his own.

"Hi," Audra said softly, her voice a little shaky. "We're here."

Jairo cleared his throat, trying to steady himself. "Hey... come in."

They stepped inside, and Jason gazed around the room, still holding tight to his mother's hand. Jairo knelt down to get on Jason's level, his heart pounding in his chest.

"Hi, Jason," Jairo said, his voice gentle.

Jason glanced up at his mother, then back at Jairo. "Hi," he said, almost in a whisper.

Jairo smiled, feeling an overwhelming rush of emotion. "I'm... I'm your dad."

Jason blinked at him, processing the words. "My dad?"

Audra placed a hand on Jason's shoulder and nodded. "Yes, sweetheart. This is your dad."

Jairo felt his throat tighten as he searched for the right words. "I didn't know about you until recently... but I'm really happy to meet you."

Jason stared at him for a moment, his expression unreadable, and then quietly said, "You look like Jairo Jones. I play him as my virtual character in my virtual soccer game."

Jairo laughed softly and then looked at Audra.

"Well, Jason, I am Jairo Jones."

"The real Jairo Jones," Jason whispered, unable to contain his excitement.

Jairo nodded, smiling.

"So, that means you play football in real life?" Jason asked eagerly.

Jairo grinned. "I used to. Maybe we can kick a ball around sometime."

Jason nodded, his eyes brightening. "Okay."

Jairo felt his heart swell as the first connection was made. This was his son, his boy, and he was determined to make up for lost time.

After chatting with Jason for a while and asking him questions about his life, the boy discovered the latest version of the e-soccer game that the designer had gifted him on his large television screen. The designer had wanted him to check it out and give him a shout-out on his social media. He had forgotten all about it in his anxiety about meeting Jason.

"You have version five," Jason said, awe in his eyes. "And you have it on the big screen! Can I play?" He looked at Jairo.

Audra groaned. "And here endeth the evening's meet and greet."

Jairo laughed. "Of course, you can play. Let me show you the basic controls."

He grabbed the controller and handed it to Jason, settling beside him on the edge of the couch. Jason's face was a mix of concentration and pure excitement as Jairo explained the controls, guiding him through moving the players, passing, and shooting.

Jason picked it up quickly, maneuvering his virtual team across the field as Jairo encouraged him. "You're a natural, kid," Jairo said with a grin.

Audra crossed her arms, rolling her eyes, but she couldn't hide her smile as she watched the two of them. She had to admit, there was something heartwarming about watching her son play with his father. This wasn't the formal meet-up she'd anticipated, but it felt... right.

Jason glanced up at Jairo. "Do you think I could play as good as you one day?" he asked, eyes shining.

Jairo tousled Jason's hair. "Keep practicing, and who knows? Maybe you'll be even better."

Audra shook her head with a soft laugh. "I guess I'm outnumbered by soccer fanatics."

"Better get used to it," Jairo teased, giving her a playful wink before focusing back on the game.

****

They left Jason to a single-player game, where he enthusiastically played as Jairo Jones in a hotly contested match.

"Do you see what you've done?" Audra murmured. They were standing in the kitchen while Jairo prepared sandwiches. "He's already football mad. This will tip him over the edge."

Jairo chuckled. "I didn't know the love of football was coded in his DNA. Is that even possible?"

"I have no clue." Audra shrugged.

Jairo walked over to her and placed a plate of sandwiches in front of her. "What drink would you like with this? I've got a variety of options to choose from."

"I'll see what you have." Audra moved away from him and went toward the fridge door, pulling it open.

Jairo cornered her at the fridge door, trapping her between his body and the fridge. "I don't like you keeping me at arm's length."

"I, uh..." Audra swallowed. "Don't look at me like that and give me some space. Jason is in the next room."

Jairo chuckled. "I've been craving a kiss from you."

"We can't keep this up," Audra whispered, looking at his lips longingly. "It needs to stop. I can't think when you're so near."

"Move in with me," Jairo said. "I want to see you and Jason every day."

"No," Audra shook her head.

"I'll wear you down," Jairo said confidently.

"I doubt that." Audra exhaled when he moved away. She had been primed and ready for that kiss. It took a while for her pulse to stop thrumming like a car in overdrive. The man just had to look at her once to turn her into a wanton mess. She had to conquer this.

Jairo stared at her knowingly. "My lawyer says I'm going to need a DNA test."

"You can get it done at Beckles Medical Center. We have a lab there," Audra said without batting an eye. "Or I can take a kit, do both you and Jason, and send it to the lab for results."

"Oh, cool," Jairo grinned. "The benefits of having a doctor as a lover. House calls."

"We can do it tomorrow," Audra said. "I have a feeling Jason will want to come back. It's not every day a kid finds out his father is his football hero."

Jairo smirked. "You should have told him years ago."

"I didn't want to intrude on your life. I figured you were happily married and would resent the intrusion. I didn't need the child support, and I figured I would find somebody of my own soon enough. I didn't realize that juggling medical school, residency training, and working long hours at a busy New York hospital would make it hard to find somebody to connect with on that level. Especially someone who has no problem with you having a kid already."

Jairo sat down at the counter across from her. "My divorce was finalized four years ago."

"Oh," Audra inhaled. "Was it your fault?"

Jairo nodded. "To some extent. I shouldn't have married

her in the first place. I did it under pressure, really. Her father was dying, and I promised him I would take care of Reba."

"What?" Audra frowned.

"It's a long story," Jairo said.

"We have time," Audra looked down at her sandwiches. "We've never really talked like this before. This is a novelty."

Jairo nodded. "I realize that. I was suggesting the same thing last night."

"Right, as if that would happen with our clothes off," Audra nodded. "Anyway, back to your story. You got married because of a deathbed promise?"

"Something like that," Jairo said. "Reba's crazy uncle burned down her parents' house with them and her sisters in it. Her father, Devin, my mentor and family friend, hung on for a couple of months, and then he, too, succumbed to his injuries. He made me promise to take care of Reba, and so I did. She wasn't home at the time of the fire, and she lost everything."

"Oh my," Audra whistled. "I have been jealous of your wife for so long. I thought you met her, fell in love, and married."

Jairo chuckled. "I have known Reba since we were kids. I loved her but was never in love with her. We might have had a better chance with our marriage if we had the chemistry you and I had. All I could think about while walking up the aisle was, 'This should have been me and Audra.'"

Audra inhaled sharply. "Really?"

"Really." Jairo nodded. "Our honeymoon was a disaster. She was still grieving the loss of her whole family, and I couldn't be aroused. We never consummated our marriage. I left Jamaica shortly after that, and she continued with law school."

Audra froze. She was mid-bite in her sandwich and

swallowed prematurely, causing a coughing fit that had Jairo looking concerned.

"Are you okay?" Jairo asked.

Audra wiped her eyes. "I think I heard you say..."

"That I never had sex with my ex-wife?" Jairo nodded. "Yes, it's true. Our honeymoon was a disaster. I think she cried the whole time. I bought her a house in Kingston and bankrolled her education and practice when she eventually became a lawyer. We spoke on the phone regularly, but I never found the time to return to Jamaica in the four years we were married. I kept my promise to her father, though. I took care of her."

Audra was staring at him, transfixed. "Oh, wow."

"Don't feel sorry for me—or her," Jairo said. "Neither of us were celibate during that time. Reba had her guy, and I had a couple of relationships. We had an unspoken agreement that we would end our name-only marriage when the other person wanted out. She wanted out when she got pregnant by her boyfriend. Unfortunately, she lost the baby—and him—in a car accident. Reba hasn't had an easy time of it."

"I'd say..." Audra whispered.

"My interior decorator suggested that you look at the design at my new place before she moves ahead," Jairo said casually. "I think that's a brilliant idea."

"But why?" Audra asked. "I am not moving in."

"You should," Jairo said. "That way, you won't have to run away in the early morning hours, and Jason and I can get to know each other."

"I'm thinking of a different arrangement," Audra said. "I already told you."

"Oh yes, the power couple dream." Jairo narrowed his eyes at her. "I don't want to rehash that. It makes me upset. Tell me something positive that will put me in a mellow mood. Tell me about your pregnancy—when did you find out, and how did you handle it?"

"I freaked out," Audra chuckled. "Then I went into denial, thinking the tests weren't true. And then I had to admit it, told my parents and friends... and everybody wanted to know who the father was. I kept that information close to my chest and quietly went to the States at my father's suggestion, mainly because my mother wasn't handling the news well. I had told her I wasn't sure I wanted to do medicine anymore, and there was a scandal brewing that was affecting the business. They didn't want me adding to it. Suddenly, her carefully laid plans for me blew up in her face."

Jairo chuckled. "I know I shouldn't laugh, but it's funny."

"I know," Audra smiled. "I reveled in being rebellious, and she couldn't do a thing about it. Unfortunately, after overhearing two doctors discussing a successful case they had with a toddler, I realized that my dreams of practicing medicine—and pediatrics in particular—were not just my mother's. They were mine, too. And I got back my love for medicine. Eight years passed like a breeze. I had to juggle childcare with residency. It was grueling. I got so thin. My stress response was not to eat."

Jairo looked her over. "You look fine now."

"I looked my best while pregnant," Audra said. "I had the perfect boobs then."

"You have the perfect pair of breasts now," Jairo said, his voice lowering. "But if you want to experience them at pregnancy size, we could make that happen again. I'd love to see you pregnant with my baby. This time, I'll be there for you every step of the way."

Audra looked at him in astonishment. "Stop talking like this."

"Sorry, not gonna happen," Jairo said. "I waited years to see you again. You've always been on my mind. I measured every woman in my life by your standard. When I saw you at Mingles a few months ago, I was blown away by how much you still meant to me. We couldn't even make it back to the hotel."

"That's just sex," Audra said.

"The best sex," Jairo said. "The kind of sex that starts wars, brings down empires, makes a once-rejected footballer pull up stakes and move back to his country when he hears you were here."

Audra opened her mouth. "I never rejected you. You made assumptions and—"

"Listen, Audra," Jairo interrupted. "I want to have a solid relationship with you. I want to prove that what we have is solid, not just insanely high chemistry. I think we can work. I think we can last."

Audra studied him for a long moment, her eyes narrowing as she processed his words. "You know, you're making it sound so simple," she said quietly, her voice steady. "You're returning after eight years, and you want us to just pick up where we left off."

"We are already picking up right where we left off," Jairo said. "I think we both need to find out if we can wing it outside of bed. Are we compatible outside of bed? Move in with me in the new house. It has four bedrooms and a helper's suite. We'll keep our hands off each other. We'll learn to be platonic friends."

"I'll think about it," Audra said. "We are really doing things backward. What's the saying? First comes love, then comes marriage, then comes baby in the baby carriage?"

Jairo grinned. "We blaze our own trail."

"I think this will finish my mother," Audra murmured.

"She's as tough as nails. This won't even create a chink in her armor," Jairo said. "When she married your father, how old was she?"

"Twenty-nine," Audra said. "He was a thirty-two-year-old divorcee."

"She lived some life before that," Jairo chuckled. "I figure that's why she's so hard on you. She was probably burned before—maybe by a sportsman. Have you ever thought of that?"

"No," Audra looked at him thoughtfully. "To hear my mother tell it, her life began when she met my dad. Her cousin Mabel is the one who lets me know what she got up to when she was a girl. I would have had no idea otherwise."

"Would Mabel know what her dating life was like before she met your dad?" Jairo asked.

"I doubt it," Audra said. "Mabel worked in Kingston as a helper for years until the family she worked with migrated, and she couldn't find another job. That's when she came to live with us. But I know someone who would know all about my mom's dating life."

"Who?" Jairo asked.

"Her oldest sister, Vivian," Audra grinned. "She is the family's benefactor, though it didn't seem like she would've ended up that way. She dropped out of high school and had my cousin, Wendy, then married an old man and inherited his vast wealth when he died. She sent my mom through med school and my uncle through law school and bought her parents a house in one of the nicer areas in Montego Bay. My mom grudgingly respects her because she's stinking rich, and at the same time, badmouths her because she is a poor example of 'a proper woman,'" Audra finished with a hint of a smirk.

"According to my mother, Vivian had it all wrong—

married for money, didn't live with integrity or whatever that means. She's had some interesting relationships, for sure. And she and Wendy are the only ones in the family I told about you and me from the start. They are as non-judgmental as it comes."

"You need a couple of those people around you," Jairo said. "Sounds like your mom's a bit of a snob when it comes to Vivian's life choices."

"She's not really that bad when it comes to others; it's me she is particularly critical of," Audra shrugged. "It's why she freaked out when I had Jason and why she'll freak out if I move in with you. We work in the same building; this could get touchy."

"That's why I say arm yourself with knowledge of her past," Jairo leaned forward. "There's always a reason why people act the way they do. Find out the genesis of her attitude."

Audra tilted her head, considering his words. "You mean, find out if some hidden heartbreak or scandal made her the way she is?"

"Exactly," Jairo replied, his gaze intent. "If she was burned or hurt in the past, it might explain why she's so hard on you, why she's obsessed with you marrying a doctor."

"Okay, I must admit, now that you've brought it up, it is something to investigate."

"Good luck," Jairo murmured. "Now tell me about Jason—everything. His favorite things, food, obsessions, colors. Does he have any fears, faults, or obsessions? Give me a dossier on my son from age zero to now. I will gather the rest of the information as I get to know him better."

Audra sighed. "I am so sorry we had to do it this way. But let's see, Jason was a calm, placid baby for exactly two months, and then he became a monster."

Jairo chuckled.

"Miserable and colicky," Audra continued. "At my grandaunt's insistence I took a year off from school when I had him. I lived with her in upstate New York."

"Your father's side of the family?" Jairo asked.

"Yep," Audra nodded. "Aunt Marlene was widowed, lonely. She said Jason and I gave her purpose again. So, I took advantage of her generous offer and stayed with her. Her house was on three acres of vast woodland. It wasn't exactly in the middle of civilization, so I was bored."

"I think that led me to pursue medicine again," she continued. "I finished my undergrad degree online, took my MCAT, and went on to med school. That was when juggling childcare came in. I had to move closer to school, left Jason with Grand Aunt Marlene, and visited every weekend. The weekends I skipped, I was guilty as hell."

"Anyway, I got through med school, and when I finally graduated, Jason was almost four. He'd become this curious, independent little kid, and in many ways, he'd bonded more with Aunt Marlene than with me. I think he even called her 'Mom' once or twice," Audra laughed softly, though there was a hint of sadness in her eyes. "She adored him; honestly, she's why I could've continued with medicine. She was my support system. My parents had offered to take him, but I recalled flashes of my own childhood. They were hardly around. I grew up with my nanny, Rosa. There was a time when my parents were building their medical dynasty, and I hardly saw them."

Jairo nodded. "Unfortunately, that's the trade-off if you want children and business success. Someone will get the short end of the stick."

"Yep," Audra nodded. "I almost didn't do the residency in pediatrics because of that. Suddenly, one day, I looked at my four-year-old and realized I didn't spend that much time with him."

"But you did it," Jairo said.

"I did," Audra sighed. "Aunt Marlene got sick two months into my first year. She went from a healthy, sprightly seventy-year-old to a weakened state in three months. And then she was gone. Jason and I grieved. I had to find a place near a good school, I had to vet a thousand nannies, I had to rebuild our lives from the ground up, really. Losing Aunt Marlene was like losing our anchor. She'd been the constant in Jason's life, and suddenly, it was just him and me." Audra paused, her eyes misting over as she remembered those difficult months. "Jason didn't understand, of course. He knew that the one person who had always been there wasn't around anymore."

Jairo reached over, covering her hand with his. "I'm sorry you had to go through that alone."

Audra offered him a grateful, bittersweet smile. "Thank you. It was a tough time."

Jairo nodded, admiration clear in his eyes. "You had him, derailed your perfect plans. I know that wasn't easy."

Audra nodded. "It wasn't, but I would do it again. I can't imagine my life without him. But I realize he deserves more. He deserves to know you, too. To have someone else in his corner."

Jairo's chest tightened as he took in her words. "And I want to be that for him. I don't want him to feel like he missed out on having a dad."

Audra sighed. "To answer your original question, his favorite color is boringly blue."

Jairo chuckled.

"His favorite food is ice cream; any flavor will do. He can devour a quart a day," Audra said. "Luckily, he's so active, or else I'd have an obese kid on my hands. He takes every opportunity to kick a ball. He's always running around, scraping his knees, climbing trees. I'd constantly have mini heart attacks watching him. He is... stubborn, fearless, and annoyingly opinionated. And he's obsessed with animals. He's been hounding me to get a cat."

Jairo chuckled. "I love cats. I wouldn't mind having one or two; having two for company is always best."

Audra smiled, nodding. "He has this adventurous side that I think you'll recognize. And he's sensitive, too. When Aunt Marlene got sick, Jason would sit by her bed and read to her every evening. She said he was her little doctor."

Jairo's chest tightened. "He sounds... incredible."

"He is." Audra paused, glancing away for a moment. "I have never regretted having him, not even for a moment. He's sensitive to people leaving. He'll need time to trust you fully."

"I understand," Jairo replied, determined. "Whatever it takes, I'm here now. I want to be there for him every step of the way."

Audra looked at him, hearing the sincerity in his voice. "I know you will be there for him. Jason deserves that."

"Oh, nothing can separate us now," Jairo said. "I will be the kind of father I never had. I always play for keeps."

Chapter Nine

Playing for Keeps. The turn of phrase kept ricocheting through her head in the preceding days. She even looked it up. It meant going all in, with no turning back. No half-measures, no exit strategy. Playing for keeps was about commitment—the kind that didn't waver or wait for a better offer to come along.

She was happy that Jairo made that reference to him and Jason. She knew how absolutely awful his father had been to him and his sisters. She felt a wee bit guilty now that she hadn't told him about Jason when she had found out she was pregnant. Hearing about the state of his relationship with Reba, apparently, it wouldn't have been a problem.

She still couldn't believe that all the hours of torturing herself, believing that Jairo had fallen in love and gotten married, had been futile. Back then, she had fallen into a trap of her own making. Where Jairo was concerned, she had convinced herself she was having a casual fling with a footballer. She wasn't supposed to be emotionally involved—she was a modern woman in university. Jairo would be her first, but definitely not her last. She would play the field and then settle down with a fellow doctor.

Several years ago, she tried to act cool when she saw Jairo parked outside her school library. She even nonchalantly strolled by, but her heart hammered a mile a minute. It had taken all her acting skills to affect nonchalance.

Years of practicing not to show her emotions had paid off. Her mother's mocking her for wearing her heart on her sleeve had toughened her up—well, at least on the outside. Inside, she was still the same vulnerable little girl, always yearning for approval. Deep down, she had always longed for someone who would see her true self and love her for who she was. She hadn't quite shaken that longing.

She exited the Beckles Medical Building. It was Friday. Usually, she would be cajoling Kenny to do something, but Kenny had told her weeks ago that she was only available one Friday night every other month. She was not into the party scene or prancing around town. She would rather lounge in her pajamas and play Scrabble with Camden.

Yuck, Audra thought jealously. But then again, it didn't sound all that bad. At least Kenny was settled with someone she loved and who loved her back.

Audra sighed. The weekend was stretching before her— barren and dry. She was sorely tempted to call Jairo.

She called before she could change her mind.

"What are you doing this weekend?" she asked when he answered.

"Whatever you are doing," was his smooth answer.

Audra chuckled, feeling relieved. Why hadn't he called her first, then? Did Jairo think she was going to pursue him?

"Never mind. I shouldn't have called," Audra growled.

"I was going to call," Jairo said as if reading her mind. "I've been watching the clock, anticipating you leaving work, and then I had this whole speech planned about taking Jason over and us doing something as a family."

"Oh," Audra was mollified. "Jason won't be available this weekend. My cousin Wendy borrowed him to be a model. She has a range of products for her latest clothing line for adults and kids. She usually uses her family as models. I expect to get a call any day now to model something."

"And you trust her with him?" Jairo asked sharply.

"Yes, he'll be fine," Audra said. "Wendy's boyfriend Randy has two boys near his age, and they run around and create havoc while Wendy's chef feeds them whatever their little heart desires. He usually doesn't want to come home to me after a weekend with Wendy."

There was a slight pause, and she could almost hear Jairo's smile through the phone. "So, it's just us, then?" he asked, his voice low and warm.

Audra's heart quickened. She'd told herself a hundred times that rekindling anything with Jairo would be complicated, especially without Jason as a buffer. But the truth was, part of her craved this time alone with him to see if they could try being friends.

"Looks like it," she said, trying to sound nonchalant.

Jairo didn't miss a beat. "Alright then. How about dinner tonight? No pressure, just two friends catching up… unless you're thinking of something more exciting?"

Audra smirked, picturing his mischievous grin. "Dinner's a good start. I feel a little knackered for anything more exciting."

"Perfect. I'll pick you up at seven," Jairo replied smoothly.

"I'll meet you at your house," Audra said quickly.

"Ah," Jairo said, "still ashamed of me, huh? You're afraid

of your mommy seeing me pick you up?"

"No," Audra said. "I doubt she'll be at home. She and Dad have a function to attend. I'll spend the weekend with you, so I'll drive over."

"You're spending the weekend?" Jairo sounded shocked.

"Yes, I am testing out how friendly we can be," Audra said. "So prepare the guest room."

"It's already prepared," Jairo chuckled. "This is interesting. I like it."

Audra hung up the phone. What on earth had she suggested? A mix of nerves and excitement swirled in her stomach. She was on her period, so nothing would be happening anyway, but it would still be a test of will. Lord knows she hadn't passed any of the tests she had put herself through with Jairo in the past.

She drove home, reminiscing.

Sometime in the Past

Jairo Jones was in her library parking lot. Jairo, her crush from her teenage years. She squealed inside her head and then composed her face into neutral, strolling past his car.

"Audra!" he called, just as she knew he would. She had practically sauntered past the car.

"Jairo Jones!" Her voice was carefully neutral, not too much excitement or eagerness.

"In the flesh," he smiled widely. He was so handsome. Her heart wasn't beating—it was doing a rapid staccato glide motion that was going to make her breathless.

"What are you doing this evening?" he asked, his white teeth flashing against his pink lips.

"Studying." She moved closer to the car. "How are you doing? I haven't seen you in like five years!"

Did he hear the tremor in her voice? It seemed not. He answered easily.

"Yep, it's been a while. I'm out here for my sister's wedding, and then I'll take my two months' vacation out here."

Audra nodded. "That's nice. Well, have fun."

She turned, waiting for him to stop her. What if he didn't stop her? What would she do? Kick herself—that's what. Was she acting too dismissive?

"Wait!" he called.

She almost slumped in relief.

He opened the car door and stepped out. Was it possible he had gotten taller? She widened her eyes as he stretched a bit. He was the perfect size—not too big and not too skinny.

"Would you like to have dinner after your study session?" he asked.

Yes, a hundred times, yes! she screamed in her head.

She was still processing the fact that Jairo Jones was interested in her. Little old her. He was a famous star now. Because of this inner dialogue, she didn't answer readily.

"For old times' sake," he added quickly. "I've been curious about your life since I last saw you. I mean, you're all grown up now, and for a brief time, I considered us friends."

Audra almost smiled. They were never friends. They exchanged pleasantries when she was younger, especially when walking her dog. She still couldn't fathom why he had paid her any special attention then. She had been short and skinny, with long, unruly hair that her mother had forbidden her from processing until she turned eighteen. Her dad used to say she had the classic bone structure of a model. Audra just hadn't seen it.

When she looked in the mirror, she saw a gawky teenage girl with zero curves.

Jairo, on the other hand, was a certified hot boy. He looked better than any of the teen heartthrobs around at the time.

And he wasn't just good-looking—he was nice. He actually had conversations with her while she dragged her poor dog, Biscuit, up and down the cul-de-sac so that she could chat with Jairo.

Afterward, when she went home, she would fantasize that he liked her and that they were a couple. He was the star of every fantasy for quite a few years. Even now, seeing him on the news, she still had a fantasy or two.

That's why it was baffling, even to her, when she said, "Dinner is okay, but I'm taking my books. I have two exams, and I want to ace them."

Jairo smiled. "Okay then, we can do a raincheck on that date. I don't want you to mess up your exams. When you're done, we can celebrate."

"When is your last one?" Jairo asked, leaning forward a little, his eyes locked on hers.

Audra glanced away briefly. She couldn't look him in the eye for too long. It made her feel jittery and trembly in her lower body. "Next Friday. After that, I'll be free."

Jairo nodded, his smile widening. "Perfect. I'll be around. How about we celebrate then? Properly."

She wanted to go to dinner with him now. Why had she mentioned her exams? Why was she jeopardizing a date with Jairo Jones? He'd probably forget about her soon.

"We'll see." She pulled her bag higher onto her shoulder and gave him a slight wave before turning to walk away. It was the hardest walk she had ever done. She had wanted to jump into his car and stick her tongue down his throat. She was feeling a little lightheaded and giddy just thinking about it.

But her aunt Vivian had once told her, "If you play hard to get, he will pursue you if he genuinely likes you. Girl, don't be too easy." Audra often thought back on that advice. "I wish I had somebody to give me that advice. Instead, I had to find that out on my own."

Audra had worried over and over, if she had played too hard to get. He hadn't called her, not even once. She had spent way too much time looking at her phone, willing him to call when she should've been studying.

True to his word, he had left her alone to study for her exams. She didn't get much studying done, though. She thought about him nonstop, researching him on the internet almost as much. But all the information was about his career. The guy had no personal social media pages—only fan-run ones. He was super private.

It had been frustrating. She didn't know much about Jairo Jones' present life. Did he have a girlfriend? What was his relationship with his mother and siblings like? She had seen his sister Josie around campus, but Josie didn't acknowledge her, and Audra wasn't the type to go over to people and initiate conversations. People generally mistook that as her being snobbish, snooty, and stush.

When Jairo called, she had been over the moon happy. She changed twelve times, finally settling on a low-key outfit that didn't make her look like she was trying hard. You couldn't go wrong with jeans, a shirt, and a matching headband.

Every brush of his finger, or if he looked at her too long, caused a flutter in her stomach that was hard to ignore. She forced herself to stay cool, her casual laugh disguising the thrill that ran up her spine whenever he was near.

They went to a small, quiet café in New Kingston. She didn't even remember what they ate.

They talked—no, he talked, and she listened. He told her about his training, the places he'd traveled, the times he had nearly given up, and what had kept him going. Every word painted a picture of a world she hadn't even dreamed of, yet he somehow made it all sound so... ordinary.

She nodded, offering small comments here and there, but mostly, she just drank him in—the way his eyes lit up when he recounted a victory, the way his voice softened when he talked about his family.

But the more he revealed, the more she realized he was leaving out the details she craved. He was an expert at skirting around personal topics, keeping things close enough to feel intimate yet distant enough to keep her wanting more. And she did want more—more than she'd ever wanted from anyone.

And then she blurted out, "So, how many girlfriends do you have?"

"None at the moment," Jairo chuckled. "I know this might defy belief because of my profession, but I'm not the type to sleep around."

She didn't believe that. She snorted inelegantly.

"It's true," Jairo shrugged. "Not only am I a one-woman kind of man, I'm heavily into commitment, and I take my relationships seriously." He looked at her significantly. "I wouldn't mind if we explored a relationship."

Did he just say they should explore a relationship? Did he mean it, or was it just a pick-up line?

"I don't know," Audra she said hesitantly. "You live in the UK, I live here. I am going to med school; you are a footballer…"

"And you haven't given up your dreams of ultimately being with a doctor." Jairo shook his head. "Tell you what, I like you. I like you a lot. I wouldn't mind if we spent the rest of the summer together."

Audra looked at him with her mouth open in shock.

"Stop pretending as if you don't like me too," Jairo leaned closer. "I know when a girl likes me. I feel the pull between us. I'm not going to ignore it. I'm not proposing marriage. I won't interfere with your plans of ultimately being with a doctor. All I'm asking is that we see where you and I go."

Audra was nodding before he finished speaking. "Okay. But if we're going to do this, it has to be a secret."

"Why?" Jairo frowned.

"Because I don't want my parents to find out. I can't deal with the lectures and the general aggravation."

It wasn't her parents—her father could care less, but her mother hated Jairo specifically. She didn't seem to have a problem with the rest of his family, his sister, and his mother, though she kept them at arm's length. She had a severe dislike for Jairo.

He had waved to her when she was at the poolside doing her practice cheers, and her mother had seen it. Before you knew it, she put in hedges and privacy fences and warned Audra not to interact with the new neighbors, especially the boy.

Audra had defied her, of course, when she spoke to Jairo while walking her dog. But she had a distinct impression that whenever Jairo's name was called, even in casual conversation, her mother had a look of contempt on her face. Maybe she hated footballers that badly. Audra had no clue, but she wouldn't let her mother's irrational behavior upset her chance with Jairo Jones. Her fantasy was about to become reality. He wanted to spend time with her. He felt the attraction. It was rolling off the two of them in waves.

"Okay," Jairo looked at her, disappointment in his eyes. "I'll be your clean little secret."

Audra laughed and then sobered up. "I can't tell my friends either, especially my best friend Kenny. Can you deal with that?"

"I'm not sure. I like being private, but secret is giving 'ashamed.' You're crushing my ego," Jairo said. "What if we fall in love with each other?"

"It wouldn't work anyway," Audra said. "You and I don't live in the same place, remember?"

"There is that," Jairo nodded.

"And I don't expect you to give up a lucrative career to be with me," Audra said. "Let's just focus on the here and now."

They shared their first kiss that night. She had never been kissed that way before. She was completely unprepared for the intensity of it. His hands were gentle, cradling her face like she was something precious, and the world seemed to narrow down to just the two of them, standing close in the café's parking lot. His lips were warm and soft, yet demanding, and every nerve in her body came alive. When they finally pulled apart, she could hardly catch her breath.

Jairo gave her a lingering look, his eyes dark with something unreadable. "I wasn't planning on that," he murmured, brushing his thumb across her cheek. "But it felt right."

Audra swallowed, feeling her cheeks burn. "Yeah, it did."

For a moment, they stood in silence, her heart hammering in her chest. She knew that the reality they'd talked about was still there—he'd go back to his world, and she'd stay in hers. But right now, that logic faded in the glow of what had just happened. She didn't care that their worlds didn't line up perfectly. She didn't care about the complications waiting for them.

Jairo stepped back, still holding her gaze. "Maybe it won't work," he said softly. "But tonight, I think I'm willing to risk it. See you tomorrow?"

"Yes," she could barely get the word out.

Chapter Ten

Audra pulled up at her guest house, still immersed in the memories of the past. She needed to pack her weekend bag and shower. She entered the house on autopilot, remembering her first time with Jairo. She should name this trip down memory lane the post-mortem of a relationship that never fulfilled its full potential.

Two days after their date, she was standing naked in his hotel room. They were supposed to be going on a date, and Jairo had asked her if she wanted to come over while he got ready. She was leafing through a stack of magazines on the center table in his en suite living room.

"Even the white women have more curves than me," she grumbled. "I eat like a pig and can't even gain a pound."

Jairo had come out of the bathroom with only a towel wrapped around his waist.

He laughed softly. "Audra, self-acceptance is attractive. You mention how skinny you are at least every other hour."

Audra looked around. "I didn't know you were behind me."

"I think you're beautiful," Jairo said, his voice warm. "All your curves and all your edges."

"I'm more edges than curves," Audra had said breathlessly. A lot of him was on display, and she didn't quite know where to look.

Jairo took a step closer, his eyes filled with warmth and a touch of amusement. "Edges or curves doesn't matter. You're beautiful the way you are." He reached out, brushing his fingers along her arm, sending a shiver down her spine. "And for the record, I'm not looking for a specific body type—I'm looking at you."

Audra's cheeks flushed as she tried to keep her composure. "I don't usually feel like the type that gets noticed. Not like this."

"Well," he said, his voice dropping, "maybe you're just not looking in the right mirror." His gaze traveled over her face, taking her in. "When you see yourself how I see you, maybe you'll understand."

She bit her lip, barely able to breathe with him so close. "That's... really sweet, Jairo."

"Just the truth," he murmured, his voice thickening as he closed the remaining distance between them. He reached out and tucked a loose strand of hair behind her ear, his fingers lingering against her skin. "You're more than enough, Audra. And I want you to believe it."

In that moment, it didn't matter that they had just reconnected after three days apart or that this would be her first time with him. She felt safe and truly seen, and for the first time in a long time, she didn't feel like she had to be anything more than who she was.

Gently, he tilted her chin up and leaned down, kissing

her with a slow, smoldering intensity that melted away her insecurities. As his arms wrapped around her, she surrendered to the feeling, letting herself believe—just for tonight—that maybe she was exactly where she was meant to be.

And there began their physical relationship. She had stayed with Jairo at his hotel for the remainder of his holiday. Luckily, she had been on low-dose birth control to regulate her periods, or who knew what would have happened then? She had not exactly been thinking like a rational person.

Somehow, rationality and prudence fled when she was within a certain distance of Jairo. She had to pretend as if she had not been as affected. Somehow, she had stopped herself from being too clingy, from calling him every day, from prying into his life like she wanted to. She had kept a distance, guarding herself for her own peace of mind. He had taken her casual approach as disinterest, but the truth was, she was as vulnerable as a schoolgirl with a crush, and it terrified her.

He'd always had this strange power over her, pulling her in with a single look, his presence like a magnet she couldn't resist. But she had learned early on to mask her feelings, to hide her reactions behind a cool exterior. It was the only way she could survive around him without giving herself away completely.

Why did he have this effect on her? It had spoiled her for other relationships. Anytime she attempted to get close to anyone, if she didn't feel that Jairo-rush, as she was calling it, she backed away.

That had been the sole reason for their many make-ups and breakups in the past. She had been afraid of Jairo, seeing just how deep she felt. She didn't want to be heartbroken; she had reasoned that it was inevitable, so her lack of trust had driven a wedge between them. She still remembered their last breakup conversation.

She had just finished a call with Travis Pierce. He had declared himself the group leader on a chemistry project and had taken this as an excuse to call her frequently about things unrelated to the group.

Travis was at university on a football scholarship, but he didn't fit the dumb jock stereotype. He had an eidetic memory and didn't have to study like everyone else, and he was super annoying with it. He didn't take school seriously and mocked them for being so intense about the group work.

"Let's go out to dinner, and then we can talk about school," Travis crooned in her ear.

"No, thank you," Audra growled. "Didn't you hear? I value brains over brawn. You may have an eidetic memory, but that doesn't make you smart. You're just a player. Frankly, I don't think a relationship with a dumb footballer is sustainable."

Travis had laughed. "I'm going to get you to go out with me, Audra. Your insults aren't hitting the way you think they are. I think of them as love bites."

She had hung up the phone and paced the en suite, fuming.

Jairo had come up behind her and hugged her from behind, and they had stood there for what felt like an eternity in that pose. Then he had started kissing her roughly.

She had welcomed it. Their last conversation had not been particularly pleasant. She had been trying hard not to act jealous that he had taken time off to visit a family friend, Reba, when he had never done that for her. She had made snarky comments along the lines of, I'm quite happy that what we have is not serious, and we can end it whenever we feel like it. Otherwise, I'd be jealous.

He hadn't said a word, went to shower, and now he was back kissing her like it was their last time. It was exhilarating and yet terrifying at the same time.

He had taken her to bed, and they had made love all evening. He kissed her whenever she tried to talk or ask him a question. Then, the morning after, Jairo had looked at her deadpan.

"Audra, you're right. I can't deal with this rollercoaster relationship anymore. It's affecting my mental health."

"Cool," she had said without any discernible expression.

"I mean it," he had said. "Maybe now's not our time. Clearly, your long-term plans don't involve marrying a dumb footballer."

Audra had been trying hard not to break down. She had merely nodded. She couldn't even trust herself to speak.

She had picked up her things, told him a stiff goodbye, and left the hotel room. She had barely made it to her car before she started crying.

That was their last conversation before she read that Jairo Jones was having his bachelor party in Jamaica a few months later.

She had missed him fiercely over the ensuing months of no contact. She had forced herself not to call. But she had waited for him to reach out, and when he didn't, she had finally gotten the message. It was really over.

She had been low-key gutted and lonely in her grief. She had to pretend she was fine when she attended classes and interacted with her friends. She even went to Rory and Jewel's wedding and acted as if she was happy for them. What she had really wanted to do was jump on the table and declare, love sucks! I suck! My life sucks!

She had left the reception feeling a little unhinged, pacing her dorm room, trying to convince herself that she didn't care. She had even written a Note to Self—five reasons why Jairo Jones and I are not meant to be. Number one: he isn't a doctor. Number two: he doesn't love me. Number three: we weren't meant to be. Number four: we have nothing in common but sex. Number five: he chose someone else. That last one had stung the worst, and she'd circled it three times, as if somehow underlining the words would make them sink in, would force her heart to finally let go. But no matter how hard she tried, she couldn't shake the memories of him. Every smile, every laugh, every touch haunted her.

Despite her best efforts, she couldn't stop thinking about the way he'd looked at her that morning, the weight in his eyes when he said it was affecting his mental health. Part of her wanted to hate him for making her feel like she was the problem. But deep down, she knew it was more complicated than that. They had been an impossible equation from the start, at least in her head. Both of them had held back from the other, not wanting to be vulnerable or hurt.

She would rectify that now. She would go to his hotel and lay it on the line. She would tell him how she really felt and beg him not to get married, promising him that she would change and show him the real her. None of that had happened. She had entered the lobby of his hotel when he was heading toward the bank of elevators to go up to his room.

He looked sad. He didn't look like a man who was about to get married to the love of his life.

She had slowed down in his line of sight, and he had looked across at her. She didn't know if he had been surprised. They stood looking at each other, and then he said, "Come here."

That had been all the words spoken between them that night. She had gone to him like a homing pigeon finding its way back, and he'd wrapped his arms around her with a sense of urgency and desperation that mirrored her own. They hadn't needed words; the touch of his hand on her back and his face pressed against her hair spoke of everything unspoken between them. She had melted into him, letting all the defenses she'd built up over the months fall away in quiet surrender.

Upstairs, they'd drifted into his room, both silent, both knowing that this might be the last time. He held her as though he'd been holding his breath since the day they'd parted, and in the darkness, they found a language that didn't rely on promises or apologies. All that mattered was that they were together, at least for now, in this fragile, fleeting moment.

But by morning, reality had seeped back in. They lay tangled in the sheets, his hand tracing small circles on her back, his gaze distant and contemplative. She had known what was coming even before he spoke.

"Last night…" he began, his voice thick with emotion. "It was a reminder of how much we could be. But it doesn't change anything, Audra. I can't keep doing this, hoping things will fall into place, only for us to end up right back here. Besides, I am getting married today."

Her heart sank, the weight of his words pressing down on her. She wanted to argue, to plead, but she'd already known this was coming. She'd felt it the moment she saw that look in his eyes the night before.

"Still?" she whispered, her voice steady despite the ache inside. "Didn't last night change anything?"

"No," he replied, getting up. "I have to marry Reba. Everything is in place."

Audra searched for words, but nothing seemed strong enough to break through the wall he'd put up. She wrapped the sheets tighter around herself, fighting back the sting of rejection. "So that's it?" she managed to say, her voice trembling despite her best efforts to stay calm. "We just pretend last night never happened?"

He paused, glancing back at her, and for a moment, she thought she saw a flicker of regret in his eyes. "Audra…" he sighed, running a hand through his hair. "I promised her father I would do this on his death bed. It's too late to turn back now."

She forced herself to nod, her throat tight. She had known this might happen and she'd braced herself for it, but hearing him say it, seeing him prepare to walk away, made the reality shatter her heart all over again. "Then… I guess this is goodbye," she whispered, her voice barely audible.

Jairo nodded, pain flashing briefly in his eyes before he turned away. "I'm going to shower," he said, moving toward the bathroom door. With one last look, he left the room.

When the door clicked shut, Audra barely held back from letting herself break down. She was still in his hotel room. She needed to be alone in her dorm. She would turn the music up loud and wail like a madwoman because it was over. Really over. And this time, she knew there was no going back.

****

"What do you mean you want to quit medicine?" Her mother had screeched down the phone when Audra had finally mustered the courage to tell her about her pregnancy. She had deliberately led with the "quit medicine" bit to take the sting away from the pregnancy news.

She had calculated it just right—her mother hadn't even registered the pregnancy part.

"Final-year biochemistry student quits!" Anastasia bellowed. "For what?"

"Because I am pregnant," Audra said.

"Pregnancies can be terminated," Anastasia said coldly.

"I don't want to," Audra said. "I love kids. I want at least four."

She heard a hissing sound. She imagined it was steam escaping from her mother's ears.

"We had a plan," Anastasia said. "You do your first degree, med school, and residency in whatever area your heart desires. Then you marry a fellow doctor, join the family practice, and have kids."

Her mother sounded broken. Audra felt a pang of regret for derailing her mother's plan.

And then her father came on the phone and said gruffly, "What's this I hear about me becoming a grandfather? My baby is having a baby—congrats, kid."

Audra almost wept in relief. Finally, some positivity. She had been in denial about her pregnancy for so long.

"Thanks, Dad," she choked out, feeling a flood of gratitude. Her father's support was like a balm, soothing her frayed nerves. She'd known telling her mother would be a challenge, but she hadn't anticipated just how relentless the pressure would be to follow the predetermined path. Her father, though, had always been her ally—the steady presence who saw her dreams as her own.

"I don't understand why you're encouraging this," her mother snapped, her voice tight with disappointment. "She's throwing everything away for a… a…"

"For a child," her father interrupted, his tone firm. "Our grandchild. And if that's her choice, we'll stand by it. She's worked hard enough her whole life; she can choose her own path."

There was a tense silence before her mother spoke again, this time quieter but no less disapproving.

"Who is the father, Audra?"

"He is not in the picture," Audra swallowed.

"Why isn't he in the picture?" Anastasia demanded. "Who is he? A fellow student? Were you raped?"

"No to all of the above," Audra said. "I am not telling you who it is, so you can stop asking."

"That's it!" Anastasia fumed. "If you don't tell me who it is, little rich girl, your money train is over. Who will bankroll you with that attitude?"

"Come on, Ana," her father murmured. "We are not turning our backs on our child because she doesn't want to tell us who the father is."

"Oh no, we are not turning our backs on Audra. She needs to tell us who the father is, and we'll work something out."

"I won't say," Audra said stubbornly. "And I don't care how much you want to threaten me."

"You are only acting like this because your father is a big old softie, and you know he won't leave you destitute!" Ana said. "But I don't care what your father says—you can't come back here, unmarried, with no father for your baby in sight. Stay in Kingston, hide away. Let me have some dignity."

"That is such an old-fashioned attitude," Audra snorted. "Are you sure we're still living in the twenty-first century?"

"Maybe if I didn't brag so much about you, I could endure this with dignity," Anastasia sighed. "As the situation is, I will not be able to hold up my head in the medical community when this news spreads. Not at this moment. This can affect our business."

"How?" Audra asked. "How will my private life affect your business? Nobody even knows me."

"Unfortunately, as extreme as it sounds," Samuel murmured, "Beckles Medical is a hotbed of gossip at the moment. This will only add to it."

"What gossip?" Audra asked.

"Well..." her father hesitated, clearly torn about revealing the details. "There's talk about a certain inappropriate relationship between a partner on staff and a pregnant teen. He denies there is a sexual relationship, but the girl insists there was."

Audra listened in shock. "You're kidding. A scandal like that... Who would even believe something like that could go on at Beckles Medical? Who is it? It's Dr. Fuller, isn't it?"

"And that's the point," Samuel said. "That's what we battle with—the curiosity, the judgments. And it's not just about what's true; it's about perception. We've built a reputation for integrity, for providing care in a way people trust. And now, with this... people are talking. Even if it's all hearsay, it's already affecting business."

Anastasia added sharply, "The last thing we need right now is more fuel for the rumor mill. You showing up visibly pregnant with no father in tow would cause talk and speculation about your child—"

"Ana," Samuel interrupted. "Let's stick to the point. Audra, we are not asking you to hide, but you must understand that anything that feeds into the gossip only makes things harder for us. People love to find something salacious, and we're in a position where even a whisper has an impact. We don't want a pile-up of gossip relating to the business at the same time. Could you please stay with your Aunt Marlene in New York until everything cools off? I'll work everything out with her; she's hinted that she wants company. This would be perfect."

"Okay," Audra said. "But I am only doing it because Dad asked nicely. And I am not really keen on having people gossip about me and my baby's father anyway."

Chapter Eleven

Audra stepped into the shower and chose her Wild Watermelon bath gel. She inhaled the scent of it, then started scrubbing away. Nearly nine years later, here she was—mother of an eight-year-old, a woman who still had the same complex, confused feelings for her son's father. It was quite evident that she and Jairo were still intensely attracted to each other. Four months ago, at the club Mingles, a club she had dragged her friend Kenny to because she was determined to put herself out there and stop living like a nun. She and Jairo had taken one look at each other, and the low, humming desire had burst into flames.

The two of them had tried valiantly to converse while the music played in the background. DJ Duke's song, 'It's Always You,' had been playing. It's always been you, no one else will do, if you want me, don't hide it, if you need me, don't resist it, just call me, I'll come running…

The song had pulsed through the speakers, the lyrics

striking a nerve. Jairo's gaze was intense, holding hers with a look that told her he felt the same relentless pull. Audra had tried to be casual, to laugh and brush it off, but it had been impossible to ignore the heat between them.

"What are we doing?" he'd murmured, leaning closer, his voice barely audible over the music. "After all this time, why does it still feel like this?"

She had shrugged, trying to play it cool, even as her heart raced. "I would like to know that myself."

He had leaned even closer. "Let's get out of here, somewhere quieter where we can talk."

And she had nodded; she knew what he meant. They weren't going to do any talking. She had rushed to tell her bewildered friend Kenny that she was leaving. They had barely made it to the parking lot before they were kissing each other fiercely.

"The house I'm renting is pretty close to here," Jairo had said huskily. "But I feel a little out of control. What about you?"

"Same," Audra had said raggedly.

"The windows are heavily tinted," Jairo had whispered.

They exchanged a glance, a silent agreement passing between them as they climbed into his car. As soon as the doors closed, he reached for her, pulling her close. His hand slid into her hair, and their mouths met in a raw and consuming kiss. The tinted windows provided the needed privacy, cocooning them in their own world.

For a few breathless moments, the outside world disappeared, and it was just them, reconnecting in a way that felt both new and achingly familiar. Her pulse raced, her heart pounding as his hands roamed her back, drawing her closer still.

Eventually, he pulled back just enough to look at her, his

thumb brushing her cheek. "This isn't just desire, Audra. It's more. It always has been. You and I have always been dynamite together."

"I know," Audra said ruefully, straightening her clothes, feeling both satiated and hungry for more.

"Come back to my place," Jairo said. "I planned on leaving tomorrow evening, but I may just cancel my flight."

"You'd do that because of me?" Audra asked breathlessly.

"There are many things I would do just for you," Jairo said huskily. "How long are you going to be out here?"

"I live here now," Audra said. "I came back two weeks ago."

"Is that so?" Jairo started the car. "Where are you staying?"

"In my parents' guest house for now," Audra said, "until I get my bearings."

"Interesting," Jairo murmured. "If I didn't have to return to the UK by the end of the week, I would stick around."

"I thought you were retired," Audra murmured. "To hear the news tell it, it's the tragedy of the century. I swear I saw tears streaming down Randy's face when he heard the news."

"Who is Randy?" he asked sharply.

"My cousin Wendy's boyfriend. He gambles on the Premier League. You were apparently a sure winner, whichever team you played with."

Jairo laughed. "I had to retire. It's best to do it on a high."

"Why?" Audra asked.

"Knee injury. I had a minor surgery done on it a couple of weeks ago. I would have to sit out the season anyway, and my contract is up with my club," Jairo said. "I just took the opportunity to leave. Pretty soon, I'll be yesterday's news."

"So what are you going to do to occupy your time?" Audra asked.

"I have a vast investment portfolio and twelve houses worldwide. I've been on all continents and visited over sixty countries. I think I should do something I've never done or had the time to do."

"What's that?" Audra asked.

"Have a couple of kids," Jairo said. "Be a good, loving father. I know I'll excel at fatherhood."

Audra gasped. She should tell him about Jason. But not now. Maybe she wouldn't tell him. Maybe this was a ships-passing-in-the-night kind of scenario.

He looked over at her, mistaking her gasp for something else. "I'd not be averse to living with their mother and having a family life."

"What about your wife?" Audra raised an eyebrow.

"Divorced for four years," Jairo said.

"Oh." Audra held back from asking him a load of questions.

"I should have found you after the divorce," Jairo said. "But I didn't want to be hurt again. Once bitten, twice shy, and all of that."

"I didn't hurt you," Audra protested. "You hurt me."

"No, I didn't," Jairo snorted. "I was never your type, remember? I exited before you booted me."

Well, she couldn't argue with that. Audra sighed. "Let's not rehash the past."

"Live in the now," Jairo said. "I can dig that."

****

"Let's get this straight before I enter," Audra said when Jairo opened the door. "After a lengthy examination of our past, I have determined that we have a communication problem."

Jairo looked at her overnight bag, then at her set expression, and nodded. "Okay."

"We need to be friends. Nothing more, nothing less. Open and honest friendship."

"I can do that," Jairo said.

"Nuh uh," Audra said. "There's nothing in our past that suggests we can do friendship. I don't want to tear off any of my friend's clothes and sniff him like a wild animal."

Jairo chuckled. "That's good to know."

"I'm serious," Audra said. "If I keep my head around you this weekend, and we can act like civilized, normal people, then I'll even consider moving in with you at Ridgeview."

"I'll be the picture of friendship," Jairo said. "I'll treat you like a sister."

Audra inhaled. "Well, okay."

Jairo stepped aside to let her in. "I was thinking we could have dinner at the Sugar Mill Restaurant at Half Moon Hotel, but I would never take my sister there."

"Why not?" Audra protested.

"Too intimate," Jairo said. "I'd see your face in the flickering half-light, and we'd end up doing unspeakable things under the table, with both of us having a happy ending by the third course."

Audra rolled her eyes, but a hint of a smile betrayed her amusement. "So what do you suggest then?"

He leaned casually against the column in the living room and smirked. "Well, sis, it's pizza on the couch while watching a movie with terrible plot twists. Something totally unromantic."

"Perfect," she replied, relaxing. "That, I can handle."

"Good," he said. I'll go and call for the pizza, but I'll still bring out the best snacks in the house. I received a rather generous box of Swedish snacks from my friend Lars. He delivered it today. He said there are lots of 'unique treats' in there."

Audra looked intrigued. "Alright, sounds fun."

"I am a fun guy friend to have," Jairo winked.

"No winking," Audra grumbled.

"Sorry, sis." Jairo chuckled. "Do you want me to show you to your room?"

"Nope, I'll find it on my own, thank you," Audra said. She brushed past him, already feeling the familiar pull despite herself. The truth was, no matter how much they vowed to keep things strictly platonic, there was an unspoken energy between them that lingered, daring them to blur the lines again.

"And do not come near my door this weekend."

"Done." Jairo grinned.

****

They watched movies, ate, and chatted well into the night.

"Tell me, why did you name him Jason?" Jairo asked. They had turned off the television, pulled the patio curtains, and were lying on settees across from each other.

"Because he's Jairo's son, duh," Audra murmured.

"I figured," Jairo said. "It would have been better if you'd put an I in his name and called him Jaison."

"I considered it but thought it would be too revealing," Audra yawned and turned to look at him.

"Has he gotten close to any of your boyfriends in the past?" Jairo asked.

"Nope. No boyfriends," Audra replied sleepily. "I only introduced Jason to you because you're his father. There was one guy, his name was Garry. We were moving into serious territory, and I was toying with introducing him to

Jason when he got transferred to a hospital in Minnesota."

"I should have known your serious relationship would have been with a doctor," Jairo said jealously.

"Oh, come on," Audra murmured. "If you work in a kitchen, you'd probably date a chef. It's the same concept."

"Are doctors better lovers than soccer players, I wonder?"

"That's blatant fishing to find out who I've slept with," Audra threw a pillow at Jairo. "But to set your double-standard mind at ease, I have no idea. Most men don't give me the Jairo-rush. It's not worth the agro to pursue a situation where I don't have that rush. I know what it feels like, and it wouldn't be fair to subject myself to something lackluster."

Jairo sat up on the couch and stared at her. "Tell me about the Jairo-rush."

"Nope. Your head is already too big," Audra said.

"I'd tickle it out of you," Jairo said, "but sadly, there's your hands-off rule."

"Yup. Hands off. You can figure out what the Jairo-rush is. It makes me weak. Turns me to jelly."

Jairo smiled. "So, you've only ever been with me."

"Unfortunately," Audra sighed. "Of course, I have my toys…"

"I know about your toys," Jairo's voice turned husky. "Remember that video you sent me? I flew to Jamaica for the weekend after that."

"Change of topic," Audra said. "Seriously, how did we end up talking about this? I hope you deleted that video."

"I did," Jairo said. "I didn't want anyone else to see it. And I didn't want to watch it anymore after I got married. It drove me slightly crazy."

"Good," Audra murmured. "Let's talk about something else, anything else. I know! The DNA test. I brought a kit.

I'll collect a sample from you tomorrow."

"Okay," Jairo shrugged. "This is just a technicality at this point."

"Yes, it is," Audra said. "But if your lawyer says it's required, why not do it? Now, start talking about your relationships. I've been afraid to hear about them. I know all of the women are buxom and shapely."

Jairo laughed. "You know what's strange about you?"

"What?" Audra asked.

"You're obsessed with being curvy, while every woman I've ever talked to is the opposite. They usually want to be less curvy."

"It's my one obsession," Audra said. "My bestie Kenny says I should appreciate what I have."

"You should," Jairo said. "I find you just right. Can we talk about something other than your body?"

Audra chuckled. "Your other women, perhaps?"

"There weren't that many of them," Jairo said. "I was more into quality over quantity. The stereotype about sports stars having many women is flawed."

Audra smirked, raising an eyebrow. "So, you're saying you were a wholesome, monogamous football star?"

"I'm saying I never had much interest in random hookups. When I was with someone, I wanted it to mean something. And maybe I had the equivalent of the Jairo-rush. It's called the Audra-rush. That's when you low-key judge every woman based on your first love, and you tried to find something similar."

Audra gasped.

"Don't act so surprised," Jairo said. "I wanted to tell you so many times. Audra, I love you. But you kept insisting we weren't compatible because I wasn't a doctor, and all that stuff. Or that your mother would go haywire if she knew we were together."

"I never said that," Audra gasped. "Well, the mother part…"

Jairo chuckled. "I can't believe you didn't figure it out. I spent all my time off with you. I could have gone anywhere, but I chose to come out here and see you. Everybody knew that my summers were sacred. And before you say it was just about the sex, it wasn't. I enjoyed just being around you. I can't believe I'm saying this out loud."

Audra sat up on the settee, looking at him, stunned. "Well, since we're confessing… here goes. I pushed you away and acted distant, but I wanted to be close. I made little remarks like 'we're not in a relationship anyway,' or 'I'm going to eventually marry a doctor,' because I was trying to keep you at arm's length. I was too vulnerable with you. I felt like I was losing myself."

"Wow," Jairo murmured.

"I bawled like a wounded animal in the parking lot when you ended things," Audra whispered. "I went to the dorm and screamed into my pillow. I fell down a flight of stairs and broke my wrist because I was blinded by tears. I was a mess."

Jairo swallowed. "We made a right mess of things, didn't we?"

Audra nodded. "We did."

"I'm happy we cleared the air," Jairo said, his voice thick with emotion.

"Me too," Audra murmured, her heart heavy.

"I'm guessing a hug isn't on the menu at this moment?"

"Nope, no bodily contact. It can never be innocent with us," Audra said. "I have a lot to think about. I probably should go to bed."

"Goodnight," Jairo said softly, his eyes following her

as she walked away, the weight of their words lingering between them.

Chapter Twelve

It was a great weekend, Jairo texted Audra as soon as she drove off. And it had been. At first, he had found it challenging not to want to rip off her clothes every two seconds, but then he had mellowed out. He wanted Audra to trust him. He wanted them to work. Friendship with her, open and honest communication—that was the key. Most of their past misunderstandings could have been cleared up if they'd tried that from the start.

He wanted to be all in with Audra again. Even if that meant considering marriage. He was willing to explore that possibility if Audra would too. He'd give them time to build this friendship. One weekend wasn't enough. She needed more time to get to know him, and he needed the same. They were moving in the right direction.

He hadn't told his family about Jason yet and needed to fix that. So, he shared a picture of Jason in their family group chat with the simple question: Guess who?

He didn't have to wait long before his sister Josie replied: An AI version of you and Audra Beckles if you had a son.

Jayla quickly added: You as a boy, but lighter, with curly hair.

His mother, however, didn't take the news lightly. What the hell is this, Jairo? Don't play with me. Is this a real child?

Jairo chuckled. That didn't go down too well.

He texted back: Josie is right, except the child is not AI. His name is Jason. He's Audra's son. Just found out about him.

Before he could even finish typing, his phone rang. It was his mother.

"What?" Marshalee shouted, her voice high with disbelief.

"That was fast," Jairo said. "Hello, Mother. How are you?"

"Surprised. Shocked," Marshalee muttered, clearly thrown off balance. "How old is Jason?"

"Eight," Jairo said.

"Disgraceful!" Marshalee fumed. "Why did Audra Beckles hide this from you?"

Jairo sighed, leaning back against the couch. "I got married to Reba the day after he was conceived. I didn't want to go through with the wedding, remember? You insisted. I told you I had spent the night with someone else, and I was pretty sure Reba and I wouldn't work out. I told you I had no feelings for her, apart from friendship. And you said I had a promise to Devin to fulfill. You literally pushed me into that church."

"Oh," Marshalee deflated, her anger replaced by a weary understanding. "Yes, I remember that. You could have said something though—like that you already had a relationship with Audra and that you loved her."

"I didn't have a relationship with Audra at the time, but

I did love her," Jairo said. "Still do, to be honest. What we had was complicated."

"I'd say!" Marshalee whistled, the gravity of the situation settling in. "This news of a son must have come as a shock."

"It did," Jairo sighed, rubbing his forehead. "But I'm working through it."

Marshalee paused before asking, "Does her evil witch of a snobbish mother know that we're mutual grandmothers?"

Jairo blinked at the question, a small laugh escaping him despite the tension. "Not yet, but I'm guessing that bomb is coming."

"No, she doesn't know yet," Jairo said. Audra did not tell anyone about who fathered Jason except her aunt and cousin."

"So when can I meet him?" Marshalee asked eagerly. "I'll be in Jamaica by the end of the month. The cabins are almost finished, Hans and I are so excited. You have to take Jason to see it and for us to meet, of course."

Jairo smiled. His mother and her German husband, Hans, had built an eco-hotel in Portland. It was a dream project they'd discussed for years—small, secluded cabins nestled in the lush greenery near the beach, offering a real Jamaican experience with Hans's European touch. Marshalee practically radiated excitement whenever she spoke about it. He could already picture her showing Jason around, delighted to share her new life with her grandson.

He hadn't seen the place yet. He was supposed to go four months ago, but then he'd met Audra at Mingles, and that had literally altered the trajectory of his life.

"Sounds perfect, Mom," Jairo said, "I'll swing by with Jason."

"And you'll bring Audra, too?" Marshalee pressed. "I haven't seen her in years. I imagine she has grown and matured into a fine woman."

"She has," Jairo said solemnly.

"And you two are working on things so you can be a family for Jason."

Jairo chuckled. It wasn't a question; it was a statement. "We're working on things, taking it slow. We decided to be friends for the time being."

"Jairo Jones, I'm so proud of you," Marshalee said, her voice full of emotion. "I know this wasn't how you planned things, but look—there's still time to build that family."

Jairo swallowed, touched by her words. "Thanks, Mom. I hope so."

"And for my part in pushing you into marrying Reba, I'm sorry," Marshalee added. "I shouldn't have done that. Neither of you wanted to marry the other, but Devin and I had our dreams."

"You are forgiven," Jairo said. "I have to go now. My interior decorator is on the other line."

"Oh, you've already bought a house?" Marshalee chuckled.

"I have," Jairo said. "I'll keep you posted. I'm thinking of doing a housewarming party."

He hung up from his mother and answered Kendrea's call.

"Just a reminder," Kendrea said after they exchanged pleasantries, "if you want to have your housewarming party in six weeks, you'd better ask the lady in your life to peruse the plans."

"I will," Jairo said, grinning. "It slipped my mind this weekend."

He called Audra, who answered breathlessly as if she had been running.

"Hey, Jairo, just dashed in the house, saw my mom—didn't want to do a chit-chat."

"You act like a twelve-year-old around your mother."

"I do," Audra said with a sigh. "And I'm sure there's some psychological reason for it, but I'm not in the frame of mind to chit-chat about my weekend and where I was. Uh-oh, she's heading to the guest house."

Jairo chuckled. "Audra, get a hold of yourself."

"She's scary and mean!" Audra groaned. "Oh good, she got a phone call. She's heading to her car. Saved by the phone."

Jairo laughed. "If I told anybody this, they wouldn't believe me. A thirty-year-old woman, a doctor, hiding from her mother. And, by the way, she has a child of her own, too."

While you're busy laughing, Audra snorted. "I completely forgot to ask you something. I promised Jason's teacher that his father would help with extracurricular activities, particularly football. She wanted your email address to send you communications about that."

Jairo chuckled. "I will?"

"Yes," Audra sighed, "I'm so sorry. I volunteered you without consulting you first. But could you text me the email address where she can contact you? I'll give it to her when I drop Jason off at school."

"I'll do it," Jairo said, "if you'll look over the interior decorating plans for the house at Ridgeview. I assume you know Kendrea Carter's number. She wants to get started."

"I do know Kendrea's number," Audra muttered. "Is this blackmail? Tit for tat—you won't help with Jason's extracurriculars if I don't look at your design plans?"

"No," Jairo said, grinning. "I'm excited about doing something with Jason at school and being publicly acknowledged as his father. But I also need you to be okay with the design of our future residence." He paused momentarily and added, "By the way, when can we adjust the birth certificate so that my name is listed as his father, and he'll become Jason Jones?"

"I don't know," Audra said, her tone slightly defensive. "Ask your lawyer."

"I will," Jairo murmured. "Call Kendrea today."

"Okay, fine," Audra muttered, clearly resigned.

****

Audra had a hectic week. It seemed like all her little patients had the same stomach bug, and she was run off her feet to the point where she began to ask herself, Why was she doing this again? She found no joy in her career. This had always been her mother's dream for her rather than her own. Like now, this Wednesday afternoon, she would rather go to the school to pick up her son.

Instead, she had to call Mabel once again to do it.

"I can't this evening," Mabel said regretfully. "I have some things to do for your mother."

Audra sighed. Maybe she would ask Jairo instead. They had not had a conversation since the weekend—just random texts checking in on each other.

"Sure, I'll do the school pick-ups," Jairo said. "It's no problem. I'll even keep him after school until you can get here. I'm slated to do coaching on Thursdays anyway. I would have picked him up tomorrow."

Audra chuckled in relief. "Thank you."

"It's no problem, Audra. I'll pull my weight. I'm his father. By the way, thank you for running through the designs with Kendrea. She said your input was invaluable."

"Oh, it was nothing," Audra replied. "She sent me her plans, and I sent her my Pinterest page with all my fantasy ideas locked and loaded. She was quite happy with that. I have to go; they're paging me for an emergency."

She hung up quickly and headed to her office.

As Audra rushed to handle the emergency, her mind whirred with the chaos of the week. She couldn't help but feel a little overwhelmed. She was not cut out for this—she knew it during her residency and med school, but she did it anyway. The constant demands and unending pressures felt like they were swallowing her whole. The strain had started to outweigh the rewards.

The emergency was a young girl with dehydration, likely from the same stomach bug going around. Audra moved quickly and efficiently, ensuring the little one was stabilized and reassuring the parents that their child would be fine. Her exhaustion was bone-deep, but it was the kind of day where there was no time to dwell on it.

Finally, hours later, her shift ended. She leaned against her office chair, closing her eyes for a brief moment.

Then her phone pinged with a message from Jairo: "Hang in there, sis," with a monkey hanging on a tree, a banana in one hand.

A smile broke through her exhaustion. She texted back, "I wish I had the banana. I haven't eaten all day. I'm going to the cafeteria."

"Come back here, I'll make dinner."

"Okay, I didn't know you could cook," Audra texted.

"I can help myself. Besides, steamed fish is not hard."

Audra smiled. Now, this, she would have to see.

She exited the building almost at the same time as Douglas Mitchell.

"Tough day, huh?" he said, giving her a weary smile.

"Oh, yes," Audra nodded, "I referred three patients to you, so I know your day was pretty wild, too."

He smiled, his white teeth flashing. "I kept hearing 'Dr. Audra Beckles, please report to Emergency Room One.'"

Audra smiled. "Par for the course. There are the rare lulls—the calm before the storm—and then days like today that have me questioning whether I should even be a doctor."

Douglas raised his eyebrows. "You think that way, too? What do you know—you're a kindred spirit."

Audra laughed. "Kindred spirit, huh?" she chuckled. "So, you're saying you're not here solely for the love of medicine?"

Douglas shrugged a hint of humor in his eyes. "Well, I'm here because I'm good at it, and it pays the bills. But honestly? There are days I wish I'd chosen something with a little less...chaos."

Audra nodded, feeling an odd sense of relief that someone else felt the same. "Exactly. Sometimes, I wonder what else I could've done. I mean, I've never allowed myself to think about other paths. My mom had my life mapped out long before I could even spell stethoscope."

Douglas grinned. "Let me guess—honor roll, med school, Dr. Audra Beckles, pediatric superstar?"

"More or less," she said, rolling her eyes. "Though the 'superstar' part might be up for debate."

They laughed, the kind of laugh that only comes after a long day, equal parts relief and exhaustion. In that moment, she hadn't realized how good it felt to connect with someone who understood her frustrations.

"Well, if you ever decide to switch careers, let me know," he said teasingly. "We could start a coffee shop for burnt-out doctors."

"I can see it now," Audra laughed. "Main dish: burnt toast. I'll think about it if I survive this week."

"Are you too tired to grab a drink?" he asked hesitantly.

"I am," Audra said with a sigh. "I was heading to my... um, my son's father's house to collect him, and then I'm going to eat and crash."

"Cool," he nodded. "We'll do a raincheck on the drink."

Audra gave him a quick smile and headed toward her car.

Chapter Thirteen

"**M**om," Jason said over her head. "Dad wants to know what you want for breakfast."

"Breakfast?" Audra opened her eyes and then focused on Jason. "Where am I?"

"We're at Dad's place," Jason said. "You fell asleep in the middle of dinner last night. He took you upstairs, and then Dad and I went to get our stuff from the guest house for today."

Audra groaned. She didn't remember any of it.

She remembered dinner. Jairo had done an outstanding steamed fish. She had taken a couple of bites and then nothing.

She looked down at herself. She was in one of his shirts. She must have been out cold because she couldn't remember Jairo undressing her.

"Tell your dad I'll have what I was having for dinner. I hope he saved it for me. Shouldn't you be getting ready for school?"

Jason nodded. "I am almost ready. I need to put on my clothes and brush my teeth."

Jason left her, and Audra reclined on the pillows.

"Good morning, Doc. How are you?" Jairo stood at the door.

"Good morning," Audra murmured. "I feel as if I could do another ten hours."

Jairo smiled. "Then sleep in."

"I can't," Audra groaned. "I have back-to-back patients appointments today and my rotation at the hospital tonight. I'm not taking that on again after my six months are up."

"You have a lot on your plate," Jairo frowned. "Was it always like this, even when you were a resident?"

"Pretty much," Audra ran her hands through her hair and groaned. "It's a rat's nest up here."

"Tell you what," Jairo said, "I'll drop Jason off at school and pick him up later. I brought over enough of his things for a week and some of yours too."

"You're moving us in while I was sleeping?" Audra asked huskily. "Isn't that underhanded? Did my parents see you?"

"No, they didn't," Jairo said. "I was hoping to run into them, though. I have no intention of being your secret this time around."

"I don't expect you to," Audra said. "I just need to pace myself to handle my mother's inevitable meltdown. She'll find out about you soon enough. Jason mentions the words 'my dad' in every other sentence."

Jairo grinned. "He's a smart kid. We had fun last night playing Junior Scrabble after he did his homework, of course. Speaking of homework, what are they giving the children to do these days? I can't recall doing the things I see him doing at eight."

Audra laughed softly. "I know! Half the time, I wonder if I should hire a tutor just to keep up with what Jason's learning."

"Don't worry," Jairo said, giving her a reassuring look. "You've got enough on your plate already. I'm here for all the Scrabble games and the homework confusion. You just focus on getting through the day."

"Thank you," she said, her voice softening. "It means a lot, Jairo."

He smiled. "We're in this together, remember? Now, go survive your day, Doc. We'll see you tonight."

****

Audra was wiped out that weekend. She slept most of the time and ate only when Jairo brought food to her upstairs. Why was she feeling so utterly exhausted? She felt tired to her bones. She was so happy that she was staying with Jairo—he was the perfect host.

"I'll be getting up soon and doing something," she murmured more than once.

"Rest," Jairo urged. "There's a name for what you have here in Jamaica. It's called a body come down."

"That diagnosis sounds about right," Audra chuckled weakly.

"You don't have to work so hard," Jairo said, sitting on the bed beside her. "I'll take care of you."

"Thanks for the offer," Audra murmured, "but I can't. I was born to be busy and to have my own. Maybe I'll have to tweak my schedule for a while though."

"What's mine is yours," Jairo said, sitting beside her on the bed.

"Not legally," Audra murmured.

"We'll just have to make it legal then," Jairo said.

"Uh-huh," Audra said sleepily. "What's Jason doing?"

"Looking at some family albums with my cousin, Deanna. She's downstairs and wants to meet you, but you were sleeping, and I told her you weren't up for visitors."

"I didn't know you had a cousin named Deanna. I didn't know you had any cousins at all."

Jairo chuckled. "I have a few cousins on both sides of the family tree. My mom has four siblings, and my father has five. Most of my mother's siblings live in the U.S. All my aunts on my dad's side live in the UK. In fact, I lived with my Aunt Penny when I went over the first time."

"Uncle John Jones is Deanna's father. He has two children, Deanna and Duke. He runs a popular barbershop in Kingston, and he is an upstanding man, a loving father—the polar opposite of his younger brother, my feckless father."

"Feckless. Haven't heard that word in a while," Audra moved closer to Jairo and flung her arm around his waist. "Tell me more about the Jones family."

"Is this like a bedtime story?" Jairo chuckled.

"Mmm," Audra murmured, "Keeping Up with the Joneses."

"Well," Jairo curved his arms around Audra, "Once upon a time, in Montego Bay's most notorious inner-city, two people fell in love."

Audra chuckled. "Ooh, interesting."

"Dustin Jones saw Mara McCrae walking home from church one Sunday and invited her to his house for Sunday dinner. She never left."

"Lies," Audra murmured.

"Truth," Jairo said. "She stayed with him. He made her an offer she couldn't refuse: 'Live with me, and I'll take care of you.' Her home situation was awful, so she lived with him and bore him two children, John and Olive, and then Dustin went away on farm work, sent her his money faithfully, and told her to pay down on a new housing scheme they had in Spring Valley.

"She did that, and they successfully moved their family out of the ghetto and into a far better location. She had three children after that, with my father being the last one. They got married while Mara was pregnant with my father. He was the only one born in wedlock."

Audra chuckled. "Did it make a difference?"

"Definitely not," Jairo smirked. "He gave my grandparents a world of trouble. By the time he was born, the older children had moved out and were making lives for themselves. My grandparents had grown lax. He was fully and totally spoiled. He grew up like an only child, and they were indulgent with him. Anything he wanted, he got. His sisters were in England and would all send him pocket money. He impregnated my mother while they were in high school, and the two of them moved to St. Ann, after that my sister, Jayla, was born.

My mother was from St. Ann, and he had found a job there. He worked in construction and went to trade school to be an electrician.

"Your dad's an electrician?" Audra asked.

"Oh yes," Jairo murmured. "He has a pretty good job, too. Josie said he's a regional manager with the public service company."

"Does he have other children?" Audra asked, "Apart from you and your sisters?"

"Not that I know of," Jairo said. "At least I haven't heard anything on the family grapevine."

"And you don't talk to him?" Audra asked.

"Nope," Jairo said. "After he flung us out of the house when we were children, he completely ignored us as if we didn't exist."

"Oh wow, that was awful," Audra said.

"My grandparents, aunts, and uncle had to step in with familial and financial support," Jairo said. "And, of course, Devin, my mother's friend who was unrelated to us. Can you imagine? I remember one summer when we were staying at my grandparents' house. I was around ten at the time, and my father came by intending to stay the night. He spun around and left because he didn't want to say hello to me, his own kid.

My grandfather was sick at the time. He was so livid, he got out of bed, stood on the veranda, and quarreled about it long after my dad left. I loved my grandpa—a truly lovely man," Jairo sighed. "He and my grandma were great. They died a year after each other. I wasn't even here. I truly miss them."

"Grandparents are the best," Audra said. "My mom's parents are still around; my father's parents are gone."

Jairo nodded.

"So, when did you see your father again?" Audra asked.

"When I was sixteen. I was playing in a local match, and he was there, grinning his teeth, telling everybody I was his son. He told me, 'Good job, Jairo.' I said, 'Thanks.' And that was that. The deadbeat talks to Josie, though. She's the only one of his children that will entertain him. He uses that to pass on messages. I ignore him. He's a coward. He's too ashamed to look me in the eye, man to man, and say, 'I messed up, I'm sorry.' Until he grows a pair, I won't be entertaining him in my life."

"I'm happy I told you about Jason," Audra whispered. "I'm sorry I didn't tell you sooner."

"You know what?" Jairo kissed her on the head. "You're forgiven. The way things are going, I think we'll be fine."

"Wake me up at one," Audra murmured. I have to go to Kenny's," she slurred.

"I'll do that," Jairo whispered.

Chapter Fourteen

Audra was still not feeling energetic, but she had to show up for Kenny. She drove up to Ridgeview, and as usual, whenever she did, she admired the landscape at the front. It looked like a mini hotel at the entrance with the bold sign Ridgeview on the wall.

The security officer at the gate waved her in. She drove down a winding street where both sides were landscaped and stopped at house number one. The front of the home was designed with the elegance of a boutique hotel.

Ridgeview's luxurious townhouses exuded exclusivity and sophistication, with each of the six units styled as a mini resort. The front of the house was impeccably landscaped with tiered planters filled with colorful hibiscus, plumbagos, palms, and manicured boxwoods.

She inhaled deeply; she could absolutely see herself living here. It would be like living perpetually on vacation.

They even had a jogging trail and a picnic area. The

jogging trail wrapped around the perimeter of the complex, shaded by tall palms and lined with blooming bougainvillea and hibiscus bushes. A small, thoughtfully designed picnic area rested near the back, where residents could enjoy sea breezes while dining al fresco on stone benches under a trellis adorned with flowering vines.

Their common area was nothing short of impressive—a wide, open space with lush, manicured lawns, shaded pergolas, and cozy seating areas that felt like they belonged in a high-end resort.

Beyond the common area, Audra could catch glimpses of the sea. Stone steps led down to a private beach. She couldn't believe it when she first visited Kenny and Camden in their new place, and now she could barely wrap her mind around the fact that she could be moving beside them soon.

She had looked over the interior design of the house proposed by Kendrea, and she had not found fault with any of it. She parked and casually walked over to house number two. This could be her new home with Jairo. It differed from Kenny and Camden's place because they weren't cookie-cutter houses. House two was still modern and sleek but had a distinct personality, with unique touches that set it apart. The exterior featured rich wood accents and larger glass panels, while Camden and Kenny had stone accents.

She liked both of them, to be honest.

But did she like it enough to move in? That was the question. And was she strong enough to be Jairo's platonic friend as they got to know each other?

She walked back over to Kenny's and knocked on the door.

Kendrea opened it, a glass of wine in her hand. "Audra, you are just in time for the food to be served. What took you so long?"

"I went exploring. I've never really taken note of the other houses over here till now," Audra said. "But I am famished."

They headed to the upstairs patio, where the sea view was even more impressive. Kenny and Jewel were eating.

"She is finally here!" Kenny smiled. "Sorry we couldn't wait on you a moment longer. I asked Jill to cater, and the food smells so good."

It really did smell good.

Audra headed for the table with the food laid out and helped herself to a generous plate. The spread was impressive—grilled salmon with a honey glaze, roasted vegetables, buttery mashed potatoes, and an assortment of salads that looked like they were straight from a gourmet magazine. Jill had clearly outdone herself.

Audra sat beside Jewel, who was happily savoring a bite of salmon. "This is incredible," Audra murmured after her first taste. "Jill always knows how to make everything taste like a five-star meal. I could happily get used to this sort of lifestyle."

They chit-chatted during the meal, going for seconds and thirds. They were eating a triple chocolate mousse with a cake on top in a tall glass when Kenny knocked her spoon on her glass.

"Now that our bellies are full, can we discuss the reason for this luncheon?"

"Sure," Audra said, "but I may not hear you; this mousse is sublime."

"I'd say," Jewel said. "I don't know how Jill does it. I've had mousse before but never like this."

"Never," Kendrea agreed. "I can tell this is premium cream."

"She got it from Knightsbridge Farm," Jewel murmured.

"Knightsbridge Farm?" Audra frowned. "Aren't you

related to them?"

"By marriage, my mom is married to Phillip Knight Hastings," Jewel nodded.

"I should visit their farm shop," Audra said. "I'm going to try and make this mousse. Jason will think I'm the best mom ever."

Jewel laughed. "I'm sure Jason already thinks that."

"Now, now," Kenny said impatiently, "I have a speech planned and everything. Can I please get to it?"

"Sure," Audra licked off her spoon.

"Dearly beloved, we are gathered here today to discuss the venue options for my wedding," Kenny said dramatically. "You all will be my bridesmaids, along with Kennice and Kenisha, who couldn't make it to this meeting because of other obligations, but nevertheless, we forge on. One of you will be my maid or matron of honor.

"And before anyone asks why isn't Camden participating in this momentous decision... he was just made junior partner at Byfield and Byfield, and he is off celebrating at a football match with Rory. They've both been talking about it for weeks. I couldn't begrudge him that. Besides, he would have found this gathering quite boring."

Kendrea chuckled and elbowed Audra. "Speaking of football, how is Jairo?"

"He is good," Audra murmured.

"And you are sure you are fine with the plans as they are?" Kendrea said. "Because I am moving along tomorrow."

"Wait a minute!" Kenny held up her hand. "What is happening?"

"Jairo bought the house next door," Kendrea said. "He said he wanted Audra to live with him. I am doing the décor, so I told him to run the design elements by Audra first."

"Wait!" Jewel gasped. "Audra knows Jairo Jones?"

"Biblically," Kendrea said. "He is her son's father."

Kenny sighed. "Okay then. I guess talks of a venue will be on the back burner for now while we delve into Audra's life."

"Jairo Jones is Jason's father?" Jewel widened her eyes and then started laughing. "Oh my gosh, it's true. Once you see it, you can't unsee it. He was on the news the other night talking about his retirement. Even my happily married sisters-in-law were talking about how modelesque he looks, and he should model after this."

Audra sighed. "Okay, so the cat is out of the bag. Thanks, Kendrea."

"So, after all this time, we find out who Jason's father is?" Jewel said. "I think there should be music playing."

"You are the only one among us who didn't know," Audra said.

"I am?" Jewel glared at Kenny.

"Don't blame Kenny," Audra said. "She guessed when we went to Mingles a couple months ago and saw Jairo. I didn't exactly tell her until some time after, and even then, I swore her to secrecy. I didn't want to tell anyone else."

"Oh wow," Jewel said, but then her expression softened. "But you finally told Jairo though."

"I did," Audra nodded. "He took it pretty well. Jason is with him now as we speak."

"Have you told your mother?" Kenny asked.

"No," Audra sighed. "I'm not ready for the hysterics."

"Why would there be hysterics?" Jewel asked. "Jason is eight years old. Jairo is his father, a celebrated sportsman. Who can find fault with that?"

"My mother," Audra snorted. "My father said he knew that Jairo had been Jason's father for years, and he didn't even say a word to her. And that's saying a lot. My parents are quite close; they tell each other everything."

"Oh my," Jewel widened her eyes. "So if Jairo were a doctor, everything would be fine?"

"Yes," Audra nodded. "It would fit perfectly into my mother's plans for me."

"What about a doctor who murders people?" Jewel asked.

"Still fine," Audra said, deadpan.

"A cannibal doctor?" Kendrea asked, getting into the spirit of things.

"Once he's practicing medicine, he'd get a pass," Audra chuckled.

"A faithless, mean, abusive, angry doctor who cheats on you every chance he gets?" Kenny asked.

"Maybe he would get a pass," Audra shrugged. "I don't know. My mom is irrational when it comes to her plans for my life. Any deviation is cause for a meltdown. And like a coward, I hate the drama. The only reason why I'm not yet married and fulfilling my mother's dreams is because I, unfortunately, have never found a doctor attractive. Well, unless you count Douglas Mitchell. He's probably the first doctor I've felt the stirring of attraction toward. And I suspect it's because he has a Jairo look to him. He just came to the department, though, and it's not as if I really know him."

"She has a type," Kendrea grinned.

"I don't think so," Kenny said. "I think you just like Jairo, full stop. You shouldn't let your mother's opinions color your life. It's your life. Live it the way you want to, and do what makes you happy. She does what makes her happy."

"I kind of understand the whole mother angle to this," Jewel said. "You are your mother's only child, only girl. Back in the day, before my mother married and had twins, I was her only child. And let me tell you, she was determined that I not have a relationship with a poor man. It was crazy.

My mother grew up poor, and she was dead set against me, suffering like her. I wonder what's the genesis of your mother's insistence on you marrying a doctor—and only a doctor?"

"I don't know," Audra looked at Jewel with surprise. "Jairo asked the same thing. I'm psyching myself up to snoop around in her life when I visit my Aunt Vivian. To tell you the truth, I always assumed my mother wanted me to mirror her life. So I thought it had to do with her marrying my dad, a doctor too, and working together to build Beckles Medical Center and being a power couple. I've never thought to look beneath the dirty underbelly of her obsession."

"An obsession she passed on to you," Kenny said. "I've known you since we were three. You've always said the same thing—you're going to marry a doctor."

Audra rubbed her temples. "I know. It's like a mantra at this point."

Kenny leaned forward. "But you don't have to follow it. Your life doesn't have to be a reflection of your mother's dreams."

Audra sighed deeply. "You're right. I know that. By the way, Jairo asked me to move in with him on a trial basis to see how well we can live together and if we have something that can last."

"Do you still have feelings for him?" Jewel asked softly.

Audra hesitated. "I don't know. Maybe. I know I am highly sexually attracted to him, but when has that ever been enough to fuel a relationship for the long term? If, by chance, he loses his looks or his manhood, and if I'm paralyzed from the waist down, would we have anything to fuel us for the long term? Or the moment one of us hits a snag, would the other leave? You see where I'm going here?"

"Oh yes," the ladies nodded.

"You want a ride or die," Kenny said.

"It's like that DJ Duke song," Kendrea added. "I want a ride or die, someone who'll play for keeps, through thick and thin. I want a love that's tried and true. Stick by me, darling, and I'll stay with you."

"Never heard it," Audra said, "it must be quite new because DJ Duke is my favorite artist, but I like it. And I want what he says. That's why I'm not rushing into anything with Jairo at the moment. I may consider moving in with him, as well as I may not. Deep down, I want the traditional, societally acceptable thing of marriage and commitment. I want a man who's ready to be there for me in every way—more than just in bed, you know?"

"And with Jairo," she continued, "I'm not convinced he sees things the same way. He was married before, and he didn't take it seriously. Marriage for him has not been sacrosanct. We had sex the night of his bachelor party."

"Ooh, so he was married," Jewel said, eyes widening. "That's why you didn't say who Jason's father was."

"That's right," Audra sighed. "So I'm trying the friend route this time. He's fine with that. And we've managed to be completely platonic for two weeks. That's never happened before."

"Baby steps," Kenny grinned.

"The divorce rate is high for a reason," Audra added. "People don't stick around for the nuts and bolts of each other's lives. As soon as the going gets tough…"

"The tough get going," Kenny finished, "preach it, sister."

"Amen," Kendrea said feelingly.

Jewel chuckled. "You are thinking right."

"But how long is too long to be friends?" Kendrea asked. "How do you know when to take it a step further and move into lover territory? And what if you've kept the other person in friend territory for so long that now when you want to get out, they're quite fine with the status quo?"

Kenny looked at her sister with wide eyes. "Are you talking about Audra or you?"

"General question," Kendrea said sheepishly.

"Kendrea is planning to take Thomas out of friend territory," Jewel whistled. "Ooh, child, we should have Sunday brunch every week so I can get the latest tea on your interesting lives."

Audra laughed. "Who is Thomas?"

"Thomas Sterling, our stepbrother," Kenny answered, "Kendrea's bestie. She knew him before our mother married his father. And she's always denied having feelings for him, even though we all know she does."

"You mean Chubbykins?" Audra widened her eyes. "You're hoping to have a sexual relationship with Chubbykins? He'd crush you in bed. Can he even roll over?"

"I didn't say any of that," Kendrea said, rolling her eyes. "And please stop calling him Chubbykins."

"Yep, stop it," Kenny laughed. "He's moved way past chubby. If he doesn't do something about that weight, Kendrea will lose her man to a lifestyle disease for sure. By the way, Audra, when you move over here, Thomas will be your neighbor. Try not to call the man Chubbykins."

"Wait a minute," Audra smiled. "Chubbykins, I mean Thomas, has enough money to buy a place over here?"

"Thomas is rich," Kenny said. "He inherited his grandfather's successful business, Deals on Wheels, and has other ventures. It's well-known his mom's side of the family had money. They were frugal with it, but they're packing."

"Deals on Wheels is Thomas' place?" Audra asked. "How come I didn't know that?"

"You weren't here," Kenny shrugged. "Now enough, can

we move on to me?"

"I need to answer Kendrea's question, though," Audra said. "Remember, she asked how long is it ok to stay friends."

"I remember," Kendrea grumbled. "I was just waiting to hear your take on it."

"I think," Audra said slowly, "I would personally know if Jairo can stick around and be a genuinely friend if he can handle the ups and downs of my life without always needing to jump into bed. Friendship requires patience, understanding, and a level of respect that goes beyond romance. That's what I need to see from him first. If he's okay with that, maybe down the line we'll know when it's right to move into lover territory again."

Kendrea nodded thoughtfully. "So what's a good timeline? One month? Two years like Camden and Kenny?"

"I don't know," Audra shrugged. "My life is pretty jacked up right now. I'm exhausted. I went from high-octane residency to running my own practice. He's been there for me these past two weeks. If the guy keeps this up, I might consider one month a good trial."

"A month?" Kenny and Kendrea asked in disbelief.

"Isn't that too short to know if someone will be a genuine friend?" Kenny asked.

Jewel laughed. "I hung out with Rory over Christmas. By Easter, we were married and we've been friends ever since."

"Exactly," Audra smiled gratefully at Jewel. "Sometimes you just know, and sometimes you need a little more time. It's not about putting a timer on it. It's about seeing if he's really there when life gets messy. I was a wreck this past week, and he stuck around."

"But a month," Kendrea shook her head, still skeptical. "That seems like barely enough time to get comfortable, let alone figure out if he's in it for the right reasons."

"True," Audra admitted. "But Jairo and I are not just meeting each other, if you get my drift."

"Yup," Kenny grinned. "You have a whole eight-year-old kid, and you can't keep your hands off each other."

"That's right." Audra sighed. "I don't have the energy for games or drawn-out drama. I need to know Jairo can handle the real me, and then that's that. If he doesn't flinch in a month, we'll see where things go afterward."

"I admire that," Jewel said, raising her empty mousse glass. "Here's to short timelines, honest friendships, and knowing what we want."

The others lifted their glasses in agreement.

Kenny laughed. "Okay, well, now that this is resolved, I hope you got your answer, Kendrea. Can we now move on to me? This meeting is for me to choose my maid of honor and brainstorm the venue."

"Oh, who will it be?" Audra asked gleefully.

"I'm choosing Kendrea as maid of honor," Kenny said. "I can't choose between you and Jewel—you're both my closest friends, and I don't want any jealousy."

"Fair enough," Audra smirked. "But I've known you longer than Kendrea and Jewel; I would've liked a token consideration."

Kenny chuckled. "Trust me, I considered it. Your organizational skills are top-tier, and so is your attention to detail. I know you'd throw a bachelorette party unlike any other, but I also know you're under a lot of pressure right now. The last thing you want is to get into the nitty-gritty details of wedding planning with me."

"True," Audra nodded. "You know me too well."

"As for Jewel, she just got a promotion at work."

"Oh, congratulations!" Audra smiled warmly at Jewel. "What's the promotion?"

"VP of Programming," Jewel smiled. "I just heard last week. Unfortunately, I'm shadowing the outgoing VP and still doing my current job. It's a lot."

"So that leaves my baby sister," Kenny said. "Who has experience in planning weddings, doing the décor, and all that fun stuff."

Kendrea smiled. "I'm honored."

"So about the venue…" Audra said, "Why not get married here, in your backyard, or in the common area where the gazebo is? Hardly anybody has the kind of view that you guys have. I'd get married here in a heartbeat. It's so pretty."

"That's the same thing I said to Jairo when he was talking about his housewarming party!" Kendrea said. "Great minds think alike!"

Audra inhaled. "He's having a housewarming party?"

"Yup," Kendrea nodded. "Can you ensure he uses my friend Tiffany's catering service?"

"I don't have anything to do with Jairo's party," Audra protested. "I can't make him do anything."

"Back on topic," Kenny interjected. "My wedding is going to be huge. I've got too many siblings and step-siblings for it to be small, and most of them have children. I don't want too many people in my personal space and children running unsupervised in the backyard. I'd worry too much that some adventurous munchkin will wander to the beach unsupervised and get me in trouble. I don't want any trouble on my wedding day."

"You should use Cloud Nine Inn," Jewel suggested. "It's on a bluff overlooking the sea, with views similar to here, and they have a wedding planner on staff. That's where Shay and Jeremiah got married, and the pictures are otherworldly beautiful. I have three on my phone to show you in anticipation of the venue question." She passed around the pictures.

"It's awesome," Audra whispered.

"It is," Jewel agreed. "The smaller restaurant there would be perfect for a bachelorette party, too."

"Perfect!" Kenny said. "While you are here, can we agree on dresses? I shortlisted three styles, and Kennisha and Kenice said they'll go with whatever the three of you choose. Let's just get this out of the way."

Chapter Fifteen

It had ended up being a great weekend—relaxing and peaceful. She had gotten some of her mojo back. Audra walked into Beckles Medical with an extra pep in her step. The only fly in the ointment was the several missed calls from her mother. To be fair, she did call back, but her mom hadn't answered, which was a blessing. She expected the first thing her mother would ask would be, "Where did you spend the weekend?"

She wasn't ready to answer, with Jairo. Jairo Jones—remember him? He's Jason's father. You hate his guts for some strange reason. So, yes, she was trying to avoid having that conversation. She sure was.

She entered the lobby like a cat burglar, looking around the busy medical practice with resignation. Medicine was truly a business with guaranteed customers. Beckles Medical had three floors, twelve specialties, and a big cafeteria on the ground floor. Her mother never had breakfast there. She would be safe from seeing her if she went to the caf for breakfast. She hadn't been hungry when she left Jairo's place—not in the least—but now she felt almost weak with hunger.

Talk about her body giving her weird signals.

She furtively looked around to see if her mother was lurking anywhere in the periphery, then started walking fast toward the cafeteria. She was so single-minded in her determination to avoid encountering her mother that she bumped into Douglas Mitchell, her forehead connecting with his shoulder.

"Dr. Beckles!" he smiled. "Are you okay?"

"I think so." Audra rubbed her forehead. "How are you?"

"Great," Douglas smiled, his white teeth flashing, reminding Audra of how handsome he was. "How are you? Got some rest over the weekend?"

"I did," Audra nodded.

"So, we'll take a raincheck on our coffee house for burnt-out doctors for now?" he asked.

"I'm not sure," Audra said. "I think I may just do three days a week and share my practice with another pediatrician. A few doctors have that plan here. It works for them."

"That's what my ex-wife does," Douglas said.

"She was a doctor, too?" Audra raised an eyebrow.

"Oh, yes," Douglas nodded. "We hardly saw each other. It was too late when we both realized our marriage was on the rocks."

"Oh, my," Audra whistled.

"Going to the caf?" Douglas asked.

"Yes," Audra nodded.

"Then we can grab that drink together," Douglas smiled.

"Yup," Audra nodded. "A hot drink."

They chuckled together.

The cafeteria was bustling with early-morning activity, the smell of fresh coffee and baked goods filling the air. They threaded their way through the crowd, grabbing almost identical options—protein oats, smoothies, and boiled green bananas with callaloo.

"I see we have the same taste," Douglas said when they sat down.

Audra nodded. "Yup."

"I wonder what else we have in common," Douglas said. "Do you, by any chance, like the artist DJ Duke?"

"Love him," Audra said, tucking into her breakfast. "A friend of mine introduced me to his latest song, 'Loyalty.' Ride or die, let's play for keeps, through thick and thin, it's you I'll keep. Tried and true, no matter what we do, stick by me, darling, and I'll stay with you. It's been playing in my head all morning."

"You have a nice singing voice," Douglas said in awe.

"Oh, stop," Audra chuckled.

"I asked you about DJ Duke because I was gifted tickets to the Roundtree Music Festival. DJ Duke is the headliner for night two, Saturday night, and the person who gifted them to me strongly hinted that you were a fan."

"My mother," Audra chuckled.

"She thought you needed a break—all work and no play," Douglas said.

"She's matchmaking and you are the chosen one," Audra grinned. "Run now, get out while you can."

Douglas laughed heartily. "You are funny."

"No, I am serious," Audra said. "My mother wants me to marry a doctor and become a power couple like her and Dad."

"Your parents are outliers. I don't know how they're still together, both with demanding careers," Douglas said. "My parents are both doctors. My dad quit for several years to be a stay-at-home dad so we could spend time with one of our parents. He left medicine altogether to write books. I guess that's why he and my mom are still together."

"My wife and I were both doctors," Douglas continued. "We didn't make it. I like you, Audra, but I am not looking to get married anytime soon—and definitely not to a doctor. I like DJ Duke too, and I took the tickets because they're VIP, and I haven't been out in a while. I need to go back into the dating pool again."

Audra looked at him, stunned.

For a moment, she didn't know what to say. His honesty was refreshing, it caught her off guard.

"Well... that's pretty straightforward," she finally managed, smiling.

"Yeah, I guess it is," Douglas shrugged, looking sheepish. "I hope that didn't come across the wrong way."

"Not at all," Audra assured him. "Honestly, it's nice to hear someone just say what they want—no games."

"That's exactly it—no games," Douglas nodded. "Life's too short, and work takes up too much of our time to spend the rest tangled in unnecessary complications. At this point in my life, I'm not into anything heavy."

Audra sipped her smoothie thoughtfully. "I understand."

"So what do you say, Audra? How about we go to this festival, listen to some great music, and just... enjoy it?"

"That actually sounds good. No pressure, just good music, hanging out as colleagues."

"Perfect," Douglas said, visibly relieved. "Who knows? Maybe we'll even meet DJ Duke if we're lucky."

"I'd like that," Audra laughed.

"Well, text me your address, and I'll pick you up this Saturday night."

Audra nodded. "Okay."

****

She was packing up to leave later in the day when her mother stopped by.

"You've been avoiding me," Anastasia accused.

"Maybe a little," Audra agreed. "I did call you back once."

"I was in a meeting," Anastasia said. "I guess I should thank you for trying to get back to me. Where were you this weekend?"

"Staying with a friend," Audra said. "I slept for most of it. Didn't see half of your calls."

"I was calling to let you know I got tickets to the Roundtree Festival on DJ Duke's night."

"I heard," Audra nodded.

"Oh, Douglas asked you?" Anastasia clapped her hands in glee. "How lovely."

Audra rolled her eyes. "You practically forced him to ask me. But it's fine. I agreed to go with him. He seems like a cool guy."

"Love will bloom," Anastasia said with certainty. "He's the perfect match for you."

"He is a recent divorcee who is not looking for anything serious," Audra said. "You're way off base."

"Your father was a recent divorcee with no intention of marrying anyone when he met me," Anastasia said, "and look at us now. There's hope for you yet. I feel a perfect match coming on."

Audra forced a smile. "It's just a concert," she said lightly, hoping to deflect her mother's matchmaking ambitions. "I like DJ Duke, and so does Douglas. That's all."

Her mother gave her an amused look. "Just saying, you

two look good together."

Audra cupped her chin and looked at her mother. "Mom, I don't need you arranging my social life. I'm perfectly capable of handling things myself."

Her mother smiled and squeezed Audra's hand. "I know, sweetheart. I just want to see you happy. And there's nothing wrong with giving you a little nudge in the right direction."

Audra groaned. "Why did I have to be your only child?"

Anastasia's smile faltered. "Because childbirth is hard. Now, I have an appointment. I should get going. I'm looking forward to how this unfolds, Audra, and I'm rooting for you to take Douglas seriously."

Audra watched her walk away and then made a funny face after her.

****

She was prepping for bed that night when she decided to call Jairo. She had yet to hear from him all day, except for a text where he said he was in a meeting with his business manager. He sounded sleepy when he answered.

"What do you need a business manager for?" Audra asked when he picked up.

"I have a lot of investments and many ventures," Jairo said. "I hire someone to look after my day-to-day finances. It keeps me from getting overwhelmed so I can focus on the big-picture stuff, like enjoying my life. How was your day?"

"Great. Not too hectic," Audra said. "I accepted a date to go out with a colleague on Saturday night."

"A date?" Jairo sputtered. He suddenly sounded alert. "That's not funny."

"You and I are just friends," Audra said. "Remember our arrangement?"

"Yes," Jairo gritted out, "but I didn't know we were dating other people."

"It's not a serious date," Audra said. "My mom was trying to play matchmaker. She bought VIP tickets to the Roundtree Festival on DJ Duke's night, gave them to Douglas, and strongly hinted that he take me. Douglas asked me; I said, yes, the end."

Jairo laughed harshly. "DJ Duke, you said?"

"Yes," Audra couldn't contain her excitement. "I love me some DJ Duke."

"He's okay," Jairo said noncommittally. "He's not all that."

"He is," Audra said. "He's the full package—nice voice, handsome face, loved his wife to the bitter end, even though she was a murderess."

Jairo chuckled. "So you like a guy because he loved his murderous ex-wife?"

"He stood by her," Audra said, "until he found out she was not what she seemed and that she really committed the crimes. Many of us were rooting for Madge until we found out she was rotten to the bone. And then our hearts bled for DJ Duke. I wonder if he has someone else in his life now?"

"You are not considering being a candidate, are you?" Jairo asked, amused. "Because he's not a doctor."

"No, I'm not considering being a candidate," Audra said. "I'm just wondering if he bounced back from that painful episode. But then again, his latest song, Loyalty, hints that he did."

"Ride or die, let's play for keeps, through thick and thin, it's you I'll keep. Tried and true, no matter what we do, stick by me, darling, and I'll stay with you."

"Look at that," Jairo murmured. "You are a true fan."

Audra laughed. "I am. I just heard the song today, but the chorus has stuck."

"So tell me about this Douglas you're going to the concert with," Jairo said. "My competition?"

"He is not your competition," Audra said. "He's a recent divorcee throwing himself back into the dating world. He wouldn't refuse VIP tickets to a DJ Duke concert and was kind of pushed to take me out."

"Well, well, I'll see you at the concert with a date myself," Jairo said.

"The tickets are sold out," Audra chuckled. "Nice try."

"Not for me," Jairo chuckled. "Audra, what's DJ Duke's government name?"

"I don't know," Audra said. "I've never thought about it before."

"His name is Duke Jones," Jairo chuckled. "We call him DJ for short. He's my cousin, my uncle's son. We grew up together and are pretty close. A couple of years ago, when he divorced Madge, he had a tough time. He came to stay with me in the UK for six months, and I helped patch him up. He was in a bad way."

Audra gasped. "No!"

"Yes," Jairo laughed. "Where will Jason stay while we're both out on dates on Saturday night?"

"I, uh... Wendy, I guess. I'll have to ask her," Audra said. "I'm still recovering from hearing that you are DJ Duke's cousin. What else don't I know about you?"

"That I'm hoping we can sail past the friendship stage and go back to being lovers?" Jairo said huskily. "Right now, we could be having this conversation in bed."

"Goodnight, Jairo," Audra chuckled.

"Wait," Jairo said. "When am I going to see you again? I miss you like crazy."

"I'll come over on Wednesday after you pick up Jason from school. We'll hang out. I'll also bring by the DNA test."

"Okay," Jairo said, mollified. "Fine."

Chapter Sixteen

"I can't believe you bought property in Montego Bay," Duke Jones, aka DJ Duke, walked around Jairo's new place at Ridgeview and whistled. "I thought you would have gone for a place in Kingston, but I see why you chose to live here. The décor so far is spot on."

"Yep, Kendrea is doing a good job. Seems like she's finishing up ahead of schedule," Jairo nodded. "I can go ahead and call the party planner to do a housewarming party."

Duke nodded. "I like it. I want one. Are there any more houses available?"

"I'll call Richard Tinsdale and ask him," Jairo grinned. "I knew showing you the place would lead to you instantly liking it."

Duke sat in one of the new patio chairs and looked at the view. "Yes, set up a meeting. I'm tired of staying at hotels when I perform here in Mobay. Speaking of, I brought your VIP tickets and your backstage pass as requested."

"I didn't know you were performing this weekend," Jairo said. "When Audra called and told me she was going on a date to a show you were headlining, I was a little taken aback. I thought you were more into producing these days."

"I still do live shows if the money is right." He got up and looked at the view. "This is seriously pretty."

"I know," Jairo said.

"So, what's going on with you and the doctor girl?" Duke asked. "And what is this I hear about you having a son with her?"

"How'd you hear?" Jairo frowned. "I only told Reba, my mom, my sisters, and Deanna because she visited this weekend."

"My father is Reba's barber," Duke chuckled. "She goes to him every month to keep her fade hairstyle fresh. She mentioned it to him last week. I figured that's why Deanna stopped by."

"Of course," Jairo sighed. "She didn't say a thing though when she saw Jason. She acted surprised to meet him. Your sister is good."

Duke chuckled.

"I hope Uncle John knows I'm not keeping the news from family; this is fairly new news. I would like to introduce Jason to everyone at my housewarming party.

"Too late," Duke chuckled. "he has basically told the whole family already, including your father, who is spending his time bemoaning the fact that he's on the outside looking in on your life."

"Too bad," Jairo said without sympathy. "I thought Reba knew about attorney-client privilege. Why did she have to blab?"

"So how's it going?" Duke asked. "Are you two getting married or what?"

"Audra is keeping me at arm's length," Jairo said. "For now, we're trying to be friends. We've never tried just being friends, so she wants that. So that's what we're doing."

"You should take her to the festival," Duke grinned. "I want to meet her. And, of course, I want to meet Jason, too."

"Sure thing," Jairo said. "She's a big fan of yours."

"Ah," Duke nodded. "Then you must take her and her date to the afterparty. It's at the Palm Tree Hotel. I'll put you on the list."

"Okay," Jairo nodded.

"Any pictures of Jason?" Duke asked. "I'm kinda jealous you have a kid before me, and I'm older."

Jairo grinned and handed him the phone with his pictures of Jason.

Duke looked at the picture and whistled. "He is one hundred percent Jones."

"Yup," Jairo nodded.

Duke sat back down. "I don't know if I'll ever have any kids of my own. I always thought I'd have at least one."

"Well, why not? There's nothing wrong with you, is there?" Jairo asked.

"My current girlfriend is in her forties and doesn't want any more kids," Duke sighed. "She has three girls already, big women, all married. She's even a grandmother. It's a bone of contention with us that she has no intentions of having another child. I can't leave her because I love her. She's the one."

Jairo sat across from him. "I thought Madge was the one."

"She was the one for me in my twenties," Duke said. "And though she lied, was dishonest, and dared to be a murderer, I was truly happy with her while it lasted. I saw us living together until we were old. I was truly committed."

Jairo nodded. "I know you were."

"But then, you know what happened," Duke said. "For years, I resisted any serious relationships. I was against love and commitment, but then I met Anise, and I haven't recovered. My feelings for her hit me out of the blue. It makes what I had for Madge pale in comparison. I've never been more sure of my feelings."

"Anise?" Jairo raised an eyebrow. "Nice name. Where have I heard it before?"

"Anise Crystal Cooper," Duke said.

"Oh," Jairo widened his eyes. "That Anise. The socialite who has had several high-profile relationships and was in a very public feud with the Greystone family until they found out that she is actually Richard Greystone's love child—who almost killed her first husband, the pedophile."

"That's her," Duke said sappily. "The real Anise is quite a treat to get to know, and she is stubbornly against us going public. She wants us to remain a secret."

"Well, her life has been a media circus," Jairo said. "I haven't heard anything about her in recent years, though."

"She's keeping a low profile," Duke said. "She's a grandmother now. She thinks it's for the best."

"Wow," Jairo chuckled. "You're dating someone's grandmother."

"I know," Duke smirked. "And I want her to be as serious about me as I am about her. But Anise has been bitten one too many times. Being with her is like taming a feral cat."

Jairo hooted with laughter. "Tell me more."

"You know, when you capture a feral, you have to earn their trust slowly, one day at a time," Duke said, smiling at the thought. "You don't just march up and throw a leash on them. You sit there, and you let them get used to your presence. Every time they come a little closer, you don't push them away, but you don't grab at them, either."

Jairo shook his head, laughing. "So what does that look like with Anise? I mean, if she's this cautious?"

"Patience," Duke said, leaning back with a thoughtful look. "With her, I had to prove I wasn't just interested in the scandal, her name, or what she's done. I had to show her I was in it for her—not the stories or past. She'd test me, disappear for a bit, see if I'd stick around. And every time, I'd be right there when she came back. She's finally getting used to that."

"Sounds like you're practically living the lyrics to your latest song," Jairo smirked.

"I wrote it for her, actually. You know the verse that says: 'We've been bruised, we've been broken, left out in the rain, but I'll take every step with you through the pain. For the love that we're building, we're digging in deep, cause I don't want a moment—I want something to keep.' That lady has a lifetime of battle scars, and trust doesn't come easy for her."

Jairo looked thoughtful. "Sounds like you're playing the long game with her. I guess it's worth it, though, if she's really the one for you."

"More than worth it," Duke said firmly. "If I've learned anything, it's that love isn't about finding someone who fits perfectly from the start. It's about finding someone you want to keep fighting for—even on the hard days."

"You have a solid point. We can talk some more on the way." Jairo got up.

"Where are we going?" Duke asked.

"To pick up Jason. Audra does two nights at the hospital, and she's trusting me with him."

"Oh, great," Duke murmured. "We can spend the evening together—all three of us. Remember that 3D building puzzle Grandpa used to do with us?"

"Yes," Jairo nodded. "My best childhood memories. We'd spend hours assembling the houses, constructing the buildings, painting them, and having pure, undiluted fun. Aunt Cassie was the one who sent it from England, though. I doubt they have anything like that out here."

"That's the thing," Duke said. "I saw them at a mall downtown at a new hobby store. I almost bought it when I saw it. We could buy several of them and make a village."

"Yes," Jairo nodded. "That would be a great idea."

"The evening is about to be lit," Duke grinned.

Jairo chuckled. "No one, and I mean no one, would believe this is what it takes to get their dreamy DJ Duke excited."

Duke laughed. "It's the simple things, bro. The simple things."

Chapter Seventeen

Audra was feeling anxious when she pulled up to Jairo's house. She had left work late, had a brief nap in the early morning hours, and now, fueled by coffee, she had the school run with Jason.

When she had called Jason the night before, he had been over the moon happy. He hadn't even stayed on the phone for long. Apparently, they had been building a village made of wood. She wondered what that was about.

Jairo opened the front door and grinned at her. "Good morning, Audra. You have a whiff of fear about you. I wonder why that is."

Audra grinned. "Is my child okay?"

"Quite so," Jairo said. "I picked him up from school yesterday. We had a four-course meal, and then my cousin Duke had this brilliant idea to play this building game we couldn't get enough of when we were Jason's age. So, we went hunting for it, and the next thing you know, we were on the living room floor for most of the evening, putting together a village from the raw materials and the building plan."

"You were building with DJ Duke?"

"Yes," Jairo nodded.

"DJ Duke was here?"

"He was," Jairo grinned. "When I eventually introduce you two, can you quit the fangirling?"

"Of course," Audra said. "I fangirled over you in private. You had no idea how much I liked you, did you?"

"Not a clue," Jairo grinned.

"Well then, I'll be the same nonchalant Audra for Duke. Can I see what had Jason so excited he could barely get two words out to me last night?"

"Sure," Jairo said. "Come on in. Jason is having breakfast while examining his handiwork."

Audra stepped inside, inhaling his cologne. She closed her eyes for a moment, then got a hold of herself.

Jason was standing with a bowl of cereal in his hand, looking down at what appeared to be a small town.

"Hello, son," Audra said.

"Hey, Mom," Jason grinned at her. "Can I please come by after school and finish this today?"

Audra looked at Jairo, who grinned. "Fine by me."

Audra smiled at her son, his excitement infectious. "Well, if it's alright with Jairo, I don't see why not," she said, glancing over at him.

"Absolutely," Jairo replied, crossing his arms with a smirk. "I feel this is only phase one of the grand project. We might need a permit at this rate."

Jason beamed and set his cereal down, pointing eagerly. "Look, Mom! This is the bakery, the fire station, and the school!" He bounced on his toes, practically glowing.

Audra crouched down beside him, taking in the surprisingly detailed village. "I didn't know they sold 3D puzzles like this. This is intricate work. What's the material these are made out of?"

"Real wood. You can fit it together and then paint the buildings," Jairo said, leaning in with a proud smile. "Duke and I found a whole village, with real miniature buildings—shops, houses, and even tiny trees. We bought about six puzzles to give us a giant village."

Jason nodded excitedly. "Yeah, Mom! It's all wood! We built it piece by piece, like a real town. Duke said he's bringing paint later so I can paint my buildings however I want to!"

Audra raised her brows, impressed as she examined the intricate wooden buildings. Each structure had a rustic, handcrafted feel, with tiny details etched into the wood.

"Wow," she said, running a finger over one of the roofs. "This is beautiful. And so detailed! You know, this looks like it could be lived in."

Jason nodded eagerly. "It even has a town square! Tonight, we're adding a park and maybe some more shops. Duke said every good town needs a good recording studio, too."

Audra smiled. "I'm impressed. It's not every day my son builds a whole town before breakfast. Good job, Dad. I see I didn't have to worry about leaving him with you alone."

Jairo shrugged, his gaze steady. "I figured he needed a project to keep him focused while here. Duke and I were reminiscing about spending hours building wooden villages with our grandfather when we were boys. That was some of our fondest memories. You should have seen all three of us concentrating on our little town. I felt like a kid again. Duke almost slept over but had an early appointment, so he returned to his hotel. I managed to send Jason to bed on time, though."

Audra chuckled. "You, sir, are a natural at fatherhood. Thank you for... all of this. I can tell he's really happy."

Jairo's expression softened. "He deserves to be. And so do you, Audra."

She felt a pang at the sincerity in his eyes, but she quickly masked it with a light smile. "Well, let's not get ahead of ourselves. Let's see if this village is still standing by tomorrow."

"Challenge accepted," Jairo laughed. "And I'll make sure they leave a spot for a hospital in the plan. You know... just in case the town needs a doctor."

Audra laughed but let herself imagine for a moment—just the three of them, living in a little village. Then she snapped back to reality. "I need some tea."

"Are you sure you don't want breakfast?"

"Quite sure. Though I may change my mind later. Lately, I've been vacillating between feeling full and then ravenously hungry. It's weird. What flavor tea do you have?"

"So, we've been invited to an afterparty Saturday night," Jairo said, opening the cupboard and looking at his tea selections. "The invitation was extended by Mr. DJ Duke himself."

"When you say we," Audra raised an eyebrow.

"We, as in you and your date, and me and mine." Jairo smiled.

"Who is your date?" Audra asked, jealousy creeping into her voice.

"My lawyer," Jairo said. "She said she would be in town for the weekend. I told her about the concert, and she said she would love to come. She's also a fan of DJ Duke."

"Your lawyer is a woman?" Audra narrowed her eyes at him.

"Yup," Jairo nodded. "And she's also my childhood friend and ex-wife."

Audra glared at him. "I don't know how I should feel about that."

Jairo leaned back against the counter, crossing his arms with a smirk. "Uh-huh, but you and I are just friends, so there should be no feelings about this, right?"

Audra avoided his gaze and looked at the tea bags. "I think I want the chamomile mint. I feel a need for something soothing."

Jairo chuckled. "I'll prep it for you."

"Thank you," she murmured, feeling the heat rising in her cheeks. She hadn't expected his question to hit quite so close to home. She did have feelings about him going out with other people, his ex-wife in particular.

Jairo watched her for a moment, then sighed. "Tell me exactly what you are thinking."

Audra glanced at him. "I don't want you seeing other people, and I am especially jealous that it's Reba. Whether consummated or not, you two were married once, and I feel quite jealous."

Jairo nodded. "That's fair. Honestly, I asked her on the date to make you jealous. Just like I was jealous when I heard you were going out with what's-his-name?"

"Douglas Mitchell. He's a pediatric surgeon," Audra said.

"Ooh, fancy," Jairo rolled his eyes.

Audra chuckled.

"Last night, I couldn't sleep. I can't believe you're setting up dates with doctors while you string me along and backing me up into the friend zone."

"It's one doctor, and I'm not stringing you along. We want to see if we can be friends. I thought you agreed to that."

"We can be friends," Jairo smirked. "You slept over last

weekend, and nothing happened. We talk, and we share our thoughts and feelings. See, right now, we're being honest with each other about our feelings. If anything happens to you, I've got your back. If you need me, I'll come running."

"We are friends. Mission accomplished. One more week of this, and we could even be best friends. I've never been so upfront with anyone about what is going on in my head."

"Me too. Isn't it great?" Audra grinned. "But I was thinking we need at least a month."

"Fine," Jairo said, "as long as you're ready to move in with me at Ridgeview when it's time."

Audra swallowed a big gulp of tea and almost choked. "I'm still on the fence about moving in with you."

Jairo chuckled. "No, you're not. You know you want to move in."

Before Audra could answer, Jason walked into the kitchen.

"Mom! Can I sleep over again tomorrow night? I've been looking at the village; we'll need at least another week to finish things."

"I don't know about that," Audra murmured. "I'd get lonely. Who will keep me company when you stay away for so many nights?"

"You could come and live with Dad and me," Jason said rationally. "Then we wouldn't have to split our time between houses."

"Out of the mouth of babes," Jairo murmured.

"You put him up to this," Audra hissed, then smiled at Jason. "Let's take it one day at a time, baby. Go brush your teeth. We don't want to be late for school."

****

It was a full day, unexpectedly busy. When there was a brief lull, Audra was looking forward to a power nap in the staff sleeping room. She was lagging and feeling sluggish and didn't want to drink another coffee. She called Wendy to ask if Jason could spend the weekend.

"Of course," Wendy said brightly. "Do you have time to come over tonight?"

"My mom is spending the night, she's cooking oxtail. And I have a white knitted dress that I'd like to include in my catalog. It would look perfect on you. I tried it on another model, but it doesn't quite fit."

"Okay," Audra said. "I can't say no after hearing about Aunt Viv's oxtail."

After she hung up, a brief knock on her door had her looking up. It was her mother, looking fresh and pretty, the opposite of how she was feeling.

Why was she running out of steam so often these days?

"Mom," Audra said wearily, "I'm just going to take a power nap for lunch and see if I can recharge."

"What's this?" Anastasia slapped a newspaper down on the desk.

Audra looked down at the social pages and gasped.

The caption read, "The Handsome Jones Men." It featured a picture of Jairo, DJ Duke, and Jason smiling at the camera as they stood in front of a mall entrance.

"Good lord," she whistled.

"I knew it!" Anastasia raged. "I knew Jason looked like that man! I denied it in my head, but I knew it. That despicable monster."

"Why are you calling Jairo 'that man'?" Audra asked, confused. "And despicable monster?"

"You can't have a relationship with Jairo, Audra," Anastasia fumed. "He can't be trusted. He's a player. The whole lot of them are."

"Mom, can we discuss this at a later hour?" Audra asked sleepily. "I know you have something against Jairo, but I'm really too tired for this."

"I wish I could shake some sense into you!" Anastasia raged. "You're still seeing him, aren't you?"

"For now, we're just friends without benefits," Audra chuckled weakly. "Give me a few minutes, and then you can rage."

"No, it's okay," Anastasia said. "I don't want to talk about this again. In fact, I'm going to ignore it."

"Mom, can I tell you you're not making sense?" Audra slurred.

"Go to sleep," Anastasia said briskly. "I was never here."

Chapter Eighteen

Audra felt a little anticlimactic. Her mother had discovered who Jason's father was and had dismissed it after an initial blow-up. She went to the sleep room, closed the door, and laid on the single bed, trying to sink into sweet oblivion. But something about her mother's response was bothering her.

Her mother had said, "The whole lot of them are players." What did she mean? Was she talking about DJ Duke? As far as Audra knew, the singer was more known for his commitment to his ex-wife, Madge, who had ended up in jail for murder.

As for Jairo, he had only made the news for his football skills; there had been no mention of him in any relationships through the years. Audra knew because she had checked. She hadn't even known about his divorce. She had just recently learned that he was related to DJ Duke.

So, what could her mother have been talking about?

She wrestled with the thought, eventually worrying it to

death. She managed an hour-and-a-half nap. She had asked the receptionist for two hours and her pager alerted her that her time was up;

She yawned. Actually, she felt refreshed. But she needed to investigate why she suddenly had this lag in energy. She would do a full test at the lab. Maybe her iron levels were too low, or she was coming down with something. It was flu season, after all, and with her back-to-back patients and rotation at the hospital, it wasn't surprising if her immune system was feeling the strain.

And she might as well collect the DNA test results for Jairo while she was there. As she got to her feet and made her way to the lab, Audra replayed the words her mother had tossed out so casually: The whole lot of them are players. The phrase echoed in her mind, leaving her unsettled. What had her mother meant? She couldn't shake the feeling that there was a backstory—a web of history she wasn't privy to—that her mother knew all too well.

Who in the Jones family had her mother so upset? Because Jairo could never be described as a despicable beast.

Audra took a deep breath as she stepped into the bright, sterile light of the lab. Maybe she was overthinking things. Maybe her mother had just been angry and looking for something to lash out at.

Still, the question nagged at her as she handed over her lab orders: a full spectrum test for everything. "I'm feeling exhausted," she told the med tech, "and I'm here to pick up the DNA test results."

"Sure thing, Doc," the young lady on duty smiled. She looked at the paperwork. "Would you like a urine analysis, too? To be completely thorough?" she asked.

"Why not?" Audra replied. "Might as well."

The med tech handed her a cup. "You know the drill."

Audra smiled. "I do."

She used the restroom and was washing her hands when she looked in the mirror. She felt a sense of disassociation from herself—so strongly, it was as though she was looking at someone else. What was she doing here?

Was she really cut out to be a doctor?

What do you really want to do, Audra? She looked at her reflection in the mirror.

She leaned her forehead against the cool bathroom mirror, letting out a slow breath. She wasn't sure what had been gnawing at her lately, but something inside her was restless, unsettled. It wasn't just the long nights at the hospital, though they certainly didn't help.

It was more than that—it was the growing sense that she wasn't where she was supposed to be, doing what she was meant to do.

What did she really want? The question echoed in her head, but no clear answer came. Curl up with a book on a beach somewhere? Yes, that sounded wonderful. It sounded like freedom. She imagined the warm sun on her skin, the sound of the waves, and the quiet of being away from it all.

She was suffering from burnout, plain and simple.

****

Wendy greeted her at the door in one of her creations, a green, red, and yellow crocheted dress in the Rastafarian colors. She even had matching earrings.

"Okay now," Audra said, "you look fabulous."

"You look tired," Wendy said in dismay. "Why do you look so broken down? Where's my peppy, pretty cousin with the honey-gold skin and the long, shiny hair? Who are you? You look ashy, and your hair looks bleh."

"Shut up," Audra said, walking further into the house. "I haven't been feeling so great lately."

"Aunt Viv!" Audra called to her aunt, who was in the kitchen.

Vivian smiled and headed toward her for a hug. "You don't look that bad. Come here, my sweetie pie. Don't listen to Wendy."

Audra pushed her tongue out at Wendy, who chuckled. "I'm going to have to put on mounds of makeup to make you look good."

She hugged her aunt.

"What you need, is a little fattening up." Vivian said decisively. She looked at Audra assessingly. "I have oxtail, coconut rice, and vegetables, and you definitely need to eat some ice cream."

Audra chuckled. "I doubt that will fatten me in one evening, Aunt Viv."

"Okay, Mum," Wendy said. "Let me borrow Audra for a little while, and then you can fatten her up all you want."

The dress was hanging on a mannequin in all its exquisite crocheted glory in Wendy's design studio.

Wendy grinned. "I lovingly did it."

"It could be a wedding dress," Audra said. "I love the off-white colors, the flair at the end, and the V design at the back and front."

"I wasn't thinking of a wedding dress initially," Wendy said, "but now that you say it, I should put it under my special occasion catalog."

"I love how you love your job," Audra said wistfully.

"What's wrong, doll?" Wendy asked. "Take a load off and talk to cousin Wendy."

"I am exhausted," Audra said. "I think I hate my job."

Wendy's eyes widened in surprise. She pulled up a chair

beside Audra, sitting with a concerned look. "What do you mean? You've always loved being a doctor. You were so excited when you got into med school."

Audra ran her hands through her hair, sighing deeply. "I don't know... It's just not the same anymore. The long shifts, the pressure, the constant rush. I feel like I'm losing myself in it. And with everything going on—Jairo, Jason, my mom... it's all just a lot."

Wendy tilted her head, studying her cousin. "You've been carrying the weight of the world on your shoulders, haven't you?"

Audra nodded slowly. "Yeah. I think I've been pretending everything's fine, but I'm not okay. I feel like I'm drowning in expectations—my parents, patients, Jairo... everyone. And I'm supposed to be the strong one, but... I don't feel strong. I feel like I'm falling apart."

Wendy's expression softened, her usual playful tone replaced with a more serious one. "You don't have to do it all alone."

Audra looked at her cousin, her eyes welling up slightly. "I just don't know if I can keep pretending to have it all together. I don't know what I'm doing."

"Audra, you're allowed to be human. You're allowed to struggle. But you don't have to carry it all by yourself. Your family loves you—people who want to help you carry that load."

Audra wiped her eyes quickly, laughing a little through the tears. "I don't know what I'd do without you, Wendy."

Wendy gave a small smile. "You won't have to find out because I'm not going anywhere. But you've got to start being kinder to yourself. You can't pour from an empty cup, sweetie. Maybe it's time to rethink what's really important to you."

She looked up at her cousin. "You think I could actually walk away from my job?"

Wendy shrugged. "You can do anything you set your mind to. But only if it's what's best for you. Don't live your life just for other people. Live it for yourself, Audra. Do what makes your soul sing again. I remember giving you this pep talk when you wanted to quit school before you found out you were pregnant with Jason. And you went back to medicine."

"My mother's brainwashing was powerful, I guess," Audra said. "I am going to wash my face, then I'll be back."

Wendy nodded, watching her thoughtfully as she headed to the bathroom.

"How are things with Jairo going?" Wendy asked when Audra came back. "We haven't really talked about it since you told me you finally told him about Jason."

"We've decided to be friends to see if we can make it work," Audra said. "It's going okay so far."

"Have you told Aunt Ana yet?" Wendy asked.

"No, didn't have to," Audra murmured while Wendy started doing her makeup. "She saw a picture of Jairo, DJ Duke, and Jason on social pages. They had an outing yesterday, and she spazzed out. She called Jairo a despicable monster."

Wendy chuckled. "Aunt Ana is something else."

"I know why she reacted that way," Vivian said from the door.

"You do?" Audra asked.

"Hold still," Wendy said to her. "No fidgeting."

"I do," Vivian came into the room fully. "A long time ago, when Anastasia was working at a hospital in Kingston, she became involved with this electrician named Jarell Jones."

Audra gasped. "Jones!"

"Yes," Vivian said. "Maybe he is some relation to your Jones."

"Maybe," Audra murmured. "Is there anything else?"

"Not my story to tell," Vivian said, backing out of the room.

"Wait, Aunt Viv!" Audra begged. "Have mercy, tell me my mother's secrets."

Vivian laughed. "Spoken like a true only child. Sisters don't tell on each other. If you want to know, ask your mother."

"Fat chance of me hearing anything," Audra muttered.

"So, where are you going Saturday night? Why do you want me to babysit?" Wendy asked.

"Concert," Audra murmured. "With a colleague from work."

"Ooh," Wendy said. "Does Jairo know?"

"He does," Audra said. "And he's taking his ex-wife to the same concert to make me jealous."

Wendy chuckled. "You have to dress to the nines. I have a red crochet dress that would be perfect for you."

"Thank you," Audra said. "I wasn't even thinking about what to wear."

"Remember to mention my brand when you get compliments and tell them it's from my fall line."

"Of course," Audra said. "I always represent, you know that."

Chapter Nineteen

Audra got ready for the Saturday night concert with little enthusiasm. She was still dogged by that low feeling, and no amount of pep talk was making it disappear. She looked good, though—she was wearing the red crochet dress that Wendy had given her, and it fit like a glove. Her modest curves were highlighted in the most flattering way. She spun in front of the mirror twice; she'd also made some effort with her hair, adding barrel curls. Her hair hung a little past her waist, and while it needed a trim to even out the ragged ends, it wasn't that obvious.

Douglas came to pick her up promptly at nine.

"Wow," he whistled when he saw her. "Talk about cleaning up well."

Audra smiled. "You don't look bad yourself." And he didn't—he was in a navy-blue shirt that highlighted his biceps and fit him snugly across the chest. The shirt was paired with dark jeans and polished loafers, giving him an effortlessly suave look.

"Ready for a good time?" Douglas asked, opening the car door for her.

Audra slid in and nodded, forcing a smile. "Ready as I'll ever be."

The drive to the concert venue was filled with easy chatter, mostly Douglas filling her in on his latest work drama and random stories about his college days. Audra laughed in all the right places, but her mind felt detached, like she was watching the scene unfold from a distance.

The venue buzzed with energy. Strings of lights crisscrossed the open-air space, and the scent of roasted peanuts and jerk chicken wafted through the cool night air. A band was already warming up on stage, their music a lively mix of reggae and jazz.

Douglas grabbed two drinks and handed one to Audra. "Here's to loosening up and having fun," he said, raising his glass.

Audra took a sip; the fruity cocktail was cold and sweet on her tongue. She was about to respond when she felt a tap on her shoulder. Turning, she came face-to-face with Jairo.

He was dressed casually in a white button-down shirt with the sleeves rolled up, his dark jeans fitting him just right.

He looked at her from head to toe and murmured, "Wow, you've always looked good in red."

"Hi, Jairo." She kept her expression neutral.

Douglas stepped forward, extending a hand. "I'm Douglas."

Jairo shook his hand, his gaze flicking back to Audra. "Nice to meet you."

"You two know each other?" Douglas asked, looking between them.

"Yes," Jairo nodded.

"He's my, er… friend," Audra said.

Jairo chuckled. "Her bestie."

"Oh," Douglas said slowly, looking between them.

The air between them felt charged, and Audra could sense Douglas's curious glance. She tried not to inhale Jairo's cologne, but he stood too close.

"Well, er, where's Reba?" Audra asked, trying to change the subject.

"Somewhere around here," Jairo said, looking around. "She went backstage to talk to Duke. By the way, you and Douglas are cordially invited to the afterparty at the Palm Hotel."

"Okay," Audra said.

"See you around." Jairo nodded at them and then stepped away.

"So let me get this straight," Douglas whistled, sounding a little awestruck. "You're best friends with Jairo Jones, the Jairo Jones. The best striker of our generation. And you never said a word?"

Audra chuckled. "I didn't know you were a football fan."

Douglas still looked dazed. "I love the beautiful game. There was a time I wished I was good enough to go pro. I followed Jairo's progress through the years, half-envying him for living my dream life. He got to play on the largest stage. He singlehandedly carried Jamaica to the finals of the CONCACAF. He is the GOAT."

"Oh dear," Audra sighed. "Jairo is exaggerating. We're not really best friends. He's my son's father."

"I am speechless," Douglas said. "I had no idea you were so interesting."

"Really, Douglas?" Audra laughed. "I thought I was interesting all on my own."

"Sorry," Douglas said unapologetically. "What I meant

was, you've got layers, Audra. Intriguing, unexpected layers. Here I thought you were just a brilliant doctor who can wear the heck out of a red dress, and now I find out you were once involved with the Jairo Jones, who calls you his bestie. You're like a whole Netflix series waiting to happen."

Audra laughed, shaking her head. "Trust me, my relationship with Jairo is complicated."

Douglas sipped his drink, still looking at her like she was a puzzle he was dying to solve. "Complicated sounds interesting. And now I'm even more curious about you, Doc."

Audra rolled her eyes but couldn't help smiling. "You're impossible, you know that?"

"Maybe," Douglas said, grinning. "But you're stuck with me for the night. So, let's focus on having fun and forgetting about all that complicated stuff—at least until the concert's over."

"Deal," Audra said, clinking her glass against his.

The band started playing their opening number, Wayne Wonder's Baby You and I, and the crowd surged closer to the stage. Douglas took her hand to guide her through the throng, and Audra let herself be swept along, grateful for the distraction.

They ended up standing near Jairo and a woman with a blonde curly fade hairstyle. She wore a silver dress that exposed her legs and left little to the imagination with her generous top. Her skin glistened with glitter along her smooth, nut-brown complexion.

That was Reba? Suddenly, Audra felt skinny and scrawny next to her Amazonian beauty.

Audra swallowed, her eyes making contact with Jairo, who seemed to be laughing at her.

He waved, and she turned her back.

She wasn't surprised when she felt a hand around her waist

a few moments later.

"I don't like when you turn your back on me," Jairo said in her ear. He pulled her a little way from Douglas, who hadn't even realized she was no longer by his side.

"What gives?" Jairo asked again, his voice low in her ear.

"Stop talking in my ear," Audra said weakly.

"Why?" Jairo moved in even closer, licking her ear with his tongue.

Audra shivered. Any minute now, she would melt like a puddle at his feet.

She was saved by Reba, who stood in front of her. "You have to paw the lady in public, Jairo?"

Jairo moved his head from her ear and straightened up, but he didn't remove his hand from her waist—which was a good thing because her feet couldn't hold her upright.

"I waved to her, but she didn't wave back," Jairo grinned. "I had to find out what her issue was."

Reba grinned. "Hello, Audra. I'm Reba."

Audra managed to croak, "Nice to meet you."

"Where's your date?" Reba asked.

"Over there," Audra nodded toward Douglas. He had just realized she wasn't by his side and was looking around.

Reba waved to him, and he widened his eyes, waving back.

"I'll go keep him company," Reba said. "See you two next week. I understand we need to discuss the adjustment on Jason's birth certificate."

"What is she talking about?" Audra slumped into Jairo.

"I told her we were going to switch dates and that I wanted my name on Jason's birth certificate. You said I should talk to my lawyer. She's my lawyer."

"Oh," Audra murmured. "And why is she going off with my date?"

"To take your place, duh," Jairo grinned.

"That's so underhanded. Poor Douglas."

"The guy looks like all his Christmases are happening at once." Jairo looked over at them. "I think I just made his night. Reba took one look at him and started asking a million questions. He might have a happier ending tonight than dropping you back home with a handshake."

Audra chuckled. "A handshake?"

"Yes," Jairo said, "I would have followed you guys home, so anything else would have been awkward."

Audra laughed.

"Tonight, both couples may have a better outcome with different partners," Jairo said.

"And who says I'll be at your place?"

"I say," Jairo pulled her even closer. "I decided to call the shots. I'm amending our friendship tonight."

"How are you amending it?" Audra asked breathlessly.

"I'm throwing in some intimacy." Jairo sucked on her neck.

"You're going to mark me?" Audra said weakly.

"Good," Jairo murmured against her skin. "I want everyone to know you're mine."

Audra pushed at his chest half-heartedly, her hands trembling. "Jairo, you can't just change the terms of our agreement."

"I can, and I will," he interrupted, his voice low but firm. "No more hiding, Audra. No more pretending you're just my friend. I'm done with that. If being your friend means I must watch you go out on dates with other men, it ends now."

Her head was spinning, partly from his proximity and partly from the weight of his words.

"You're unbelievable," she said, her voice barely above a whisper. "I told you it was as innocent as can be."

"That dress is not innocent," Jairo said. "It gave me an

instant hard-on and Dr. Mitchell is human too, as far as I can tell."

"Did you get a hard-on for Reba?" Audra asked jealously. "Because her dress is even more indecent than mine."

"She was wearing a dress?" Jairo asked, genuinely taken aback.

Audra laughed. "You didn't notice?"

"Not really," Jairo said.

Audra stared at him, her heart pounding. "We're staying for the concert, right?"

"Yes," Jairo released her. She felt the loss of his warmth immediately. Her legs still felt unsteady, but she managed to take a step back, needing space to gather her thoughts and get her quivering body under control.

"We'll even maintain the status quo if you want," Jairo said. "I can go two more weekends with cold showers to fulfill your one-month no-sex rule. I just want you with me, that's all. I like it when you're around and in my space."

Audra smiled. "I don't have any change of clothes. Why don't you come over to my place instead?"

"Does this mean you don't care if your parents see me?" Jairo whispered. "My goodness, this is momentous."

"I know, right?" Audra grinned. "I don't care about anything else but being with you."

Was it a coincidence that the band started singing Smokey Robinson's Being With You?

Jairo pulled her to him, and they started dancing and singing with the band.

Chapter Twenty

Audra woke up to the sound of voices—her mother and Jairo! She looked around the room, trying to get her bearings. They had gone to the afterparty the night before. She had met DJ Duke, his girlfriend Anise, the famous producer Chex Hastings, and so many celebrities and well-known personalities that she had lost count.

Jairo hadn't left her side, not even once. She was not allowed to go off on her own. At around 2 a.m., the party showed no signs of winding down, and she was practically falling asleep on her feet when Jairo said their goodbyes.

She had fallen asleep in the car and was now in her parents' guest house. What time was it?

She glanced at the clock—just a little after 1.

Goodness, she was famished. Ravenously hungry.

She looked down at herself. She was wearing a sleep shirt. She couldn't remember coming home last night, much less putting it on.

She wondered what her mother was talking to Jairo about. Their voices sounded muted, so it wasn't a quarrel.

She dragged herself to the shower and stood under the hot water until she felt human again. Then she washed her hair. The sharp hunger pains settling into a low hum. Her fingers were trembling; she needed food in her system—stat.

She hadn't eaten much yesterday.

She pulled on a blue jersey shirt dress because it was the easiest thing to throw on; she t-shirt dried her hair and she applied some light gel to her half-wet strands. She didn't want it to dry poofy. Then she opened the door.

Her mother was talking to Jairo at the breakfast nook table. They even had food. Jairo was eating and smiled at her. "Hey, beautiful."

"Hey," she smiled back. "I must be losing my memory. I can't remember us coming here."

"Good afternoon, dear," Anastasia said civilly. "Mabel sent over brunch."

"Hi, Mom. I'm famished." She looked between her mother and Jairo and pinched herself. "I'm not still sleeping, am I?"

"No," Anastasia said. "I saw Jairo's vehicle parked before the cottage, and I brought a peace offering. We didn't start on the right foot, he and I."

"When was that?" Audra asked.

"When he was seventeen and moved in next door, I hissed and snarled at him. Have a seat, dear," Anastasia said, sipping her tea. "I'll pour the tea. It's ginger."

Audra looked at her mother wearily. "I'm too hungry to question what's happening and what you've done to my mother."

"No need to question. I'll talk while you eat," Anastasia said. "By the way, I got your medical results yesterday. I automatically opened it—it did say Dr. A. Beckles on the front."

"Am I dying?" Audra asked jokingly.

"No, you are not," Anastasia smiled. "You need to up your iron intake, though. I brought it over for you. You can assess it as you see fit. I came to clear the air with you and Jairo. Hopefully, I'll also get to speak to your mother. I treated her shabbily in the past. I was aware of who she was and was quite ashamed to look her in the eye. I think she mistook my coldness for snobbishness, but I was simply guilty."

"Yes, she'll be out in a few weeks," Jairo said.

"I remember Marshalee from high school quite well," Anastasia smiled. "She was the outgoing, life-of-the-party type. I was an introvert, always in the background."

"Wait a minute," Audra said between bites. "You went to high school with Jairo's mom?"

"And father," Anastasia said, "I had a serious crush on Jarell." She inhaled. "It was a little like an obsession, really. He was the cutest boy in school. Jairo, and of course, Jason looks a lot like him."

"Wait a minute," Audra asked mid-chew. "What are you saying? You knew that Jason was a Jones all this time?"

"Of course, dear," Anastasia said. "I figured it out when he was around three. I just wanted you to tell me."

"Good lord, you are diabolical."

Anastasia frowned. "Do you want to hear my story or not?"

"I want to hear," Audra said.

Jairo leaned back in his chair and watched the two women.

"So anyway," Anastasia continued, "I was not on Jarell's radar. And maybe that was a good thing. Marshalee got pregnant and left school. I went on to med school, and then while doing my residency at the hospital, he appeared in my life again. He was fixing a broken AC unit, and my old, unrequited crush flared up again. He didn't even recognize me. I was the one who went over to him and initiated contact."

Anastasia sighed. "We started dating. He said he was single. I believed him. I didn't know he was with Marshalee and that they lived together and had two children at the time. Your youngest sister wasn't in the picture yet." Anastasia turned to Jairo. "In fact, I think you were probably a year old. I was totally and completely in lust, and I gullibly accepted all his lies. In my defense, I was a case of arrested development socially. I had never had a boyfriend before him. I was too naïve for my own good." Anastasia looked down at her cup of tea, a shadow of regret crossing her face.

Audra paused mid-chew, her fork hovering in the air. "Wait, are you telling me Jarell Jones—Jairo's father—was your first boyfriend? And he was already in a whole relationship with kids?"

"Exactly that," Anastasia said matter-of-factly. "When I found out, it shattered me. I ended things immediately, of course, but the damage was done. I found out I was pregnant just days before, too. The whole stress of the situation caused me to miscarry."

Audra blinked, taking in her mother's rare vulnerability. "Wow, Mom."

"This explains a lot," Jairo said softly. "Your dislike for me makes sense now."

"I don't dislike you, Jairo. I never did," Anastasia replied. "I disliked that I got caught in the situation with your father, and I wanted to forget that episode of my life forever. When your mother moved in next door, I went a little overboard, distancing myself from her. She did nothing wrong. You were all victims of Jarell's callousness. I was just not ready to face my past."

Jairo leaned back in his chair, processing Anastasia's confession. "I didn't know my father had caused so much damage… to so many people," he said finally, his voice heavy with emotion.

Anastasia met his gaze. "Jairo, your father had his flaws, but so did I. I can't blame everything on him. I chose to trust him and ignored the signs because I wanted to believe in the fantasy. That's on me." She paused, her expression softening. "But I want you to know, my resentment was never toward you. If anything, I admired how well you turned out despite everything."

Audra set her fork down, her appetite completely gone. "This is… a lot to take in," she muttered. "But I guess it does explain why you were so weird when Jairo moved in next door. I always thought you just didn't like his family."

Anastasia smiled faintly. "I was protecting myself, Audra. And maybe, in some twisted way, I thought I was protecting you too. I didn't want you to get caught up in anything like I did."

Audra raised an eyebrow. "Well, that worked out great, didn't it?"

Jairo chuckled, breaking the tension. "Fate has a funny sense of humor, huh?"

Anastasia sighed. "It seems so." She turned to Jairo, her tone serious. "I want to apologize to your mother, Jairo, for how I treated her when she was living next door. It's long overdue. If she's open to it, I'd like to make amends."

Jairo nodded slowly. "I think she'd appreciate that. She's been through a lot and is in a better place now. I'll let her know you'd like to talk."

"Hopefully before the wedding," Anastasia said.

"What wedding?" Audra asked, confused.

"I—uh…" Jairo cleared his throat. "I was telling your mother that I would like to marry you soon because I find that I can't live without you for too long. I also told her I swapped dates with you and Douglas last night."

"You want to marry me?" Audra widened her eyes. "What about… you've been married before and didn't want to do it again?"

"I was clearly speaking like a man who had no sense," Jairo shrugged. "I can barely go through the day without wondering what you're doing, who you're talking to, and all of that. I'm a man possessed with the need to have you close."

Anastasia got up. "I'll leave you two to it."

"Wait!" Audra looked at her mother. "What about your insistence on me marrying a doctor? Are you just going to give that up?"

"Of course," Anastasia said. "It would be foolish of me to insist on that when you chose Jairo, and you don't even want to be a doctor anymore. My sister called me last night and gave me a good tongue-lashing about me stressing you out and projecting my dreams onto you. I didn't know you were suffering so much, Audra. I'm sorry. My advice to you is to live your life. If you want to take time off, take as much as you need."

She paused. "I would never want to jeopardize your current pregnancy in any way."

"Pregnancy?" Both Jairo and Audra said at the same time.

"Oops," Anastasia said. "Now I definitely have to leave. Your lab results are right here." She pointed to the letters and left the cottage in a hurry.

Audra started laughing.

Jairo was still shocked.

"Pregnant?" Jairo finally managed to say, his voice barely above a whisper. "You're pregnant?"

Audra wiped a tear from her eye, still laughing. "I guess so. I mean, I hadn't even read those results yet. Leave it to my mom to drop that bomb and walk out like it's no big deal."

Jairo blinked, the weight of the news starting to settle. He sat down heavily in the chair Anastasia had vacated, staring at Audra like she'd just told him he'd won the lottery and lost it in the same breath. "We're having a baby?"

Audra shrugged, her smile softening. "Apparently."

A wide grin broke across Jairo's face, his initial shock giving way to unrestrained joy. "Audra," he said, his voice full of wonder, "we're having a baby!"

"Calm down," Audra teased, though her cheeks were flushed with warmth. "I'm still processing this myself."

Jairo jumped up and pulled her into his arms, lifting her off the ground in a tight hug. "This is amazing! I don't even know what to say. First, I decided I can't live without you, and now—"

"And now I'm carrying your child," Audra finished for him, her tone teasing but her heart pounding at the reality.

He set her down gently, his hands resting on her waist as he looked into her eyes. "This changes everything, Audra."

"It doesn't have to," she said cautiously. "I mean, yes, it's a big deal, but we don't have to rush into anything just because—"

Jairo silenced her with a kiss, tender and full of promise. When he pulled back, his expression was serious. "I don't want to rush into anything, Audra. I want to do this right. I love you, and I want us to be a family. I can't imagine my life without you, not just because of the baby."

Her heart clenched, and she felt the familiar pang of fear and longing that always accompanied Jairo. "This is a lot," she admitted. "I don't know if I'm ready for all this."

"You don't have to be ready right now," he said softly. We'll figure it out together, one step at a time. But just so you know," his grin returned, "I'm not giving up. I'm all in, Audra. For you, for Jason, and now for this baby."

Audra felt a tear slip down her cheek and wiped it away quickly. "You're really not going to let me breathe, are you?"

"Not a chance," Jairo said, pulling her back into his arms. "You're stuck with me now."

Audra relaxed against him, the overwhelming swirl of emotions settling into something that felt a lot like hope. "Stuck with you, huh?"

"Forever," Jairo murmured, his lips brushing against her forehead.

And for the first time in a long while, Audra found herself thinking that maybe, just maybe, she wouldn't mind.

Epilogue

It was both a housewarming party and a wedding. Audra wore the white crochet dress that her cousin Wendy had her model a few weeks before, with a simple flower in her hair. Jairo was dressed in a tux. The wedding was small and took place in their backyard at Ridgeview. DJ Duke sang, and Marshalee, mother of the groom, and Anastasia, mother of the bride, stood together at the sumptuously catered reception and chatted. They had since resolved their past misunderstandings.

"I think they will last," Anastasia said proudly, "if for no other reason than to defy me and my insistence over the years that she needed to marry a doctor."

Marshalee chuckled. "You were ridiculous. This is a much better outcome. Jairo's the kind of man who'll always make her feel like she's the only woman in the room. That's something you can't get with a stethoscope."

Anastasia smiled softly, watching Audra and Jairo laugh

together on the dance floor, their easy chemistry undeniable. It wasn't the life she'd envisioned for her daughter, but it was certainly a beautiful one. And perhaps she was finally beginning to see the value in trusting Audra's instincts, even if it meant letting go of her own expectations.

"I suppose I can't argue with that," Anastasia admitted, watching Jairo spin Audra in a slow, intimate dance. "He's a good man, and he makes her happy. That's all that matters now."

Marshalee raised her glass. "To them, then. To love, family, and second chances."

Anastasia clinked her glass against Marshalee's, their laughter blending with the music in the background.

As Audra and Jairo continued to dance, oblivious to the crowd around them, it was clear that their journey had only just begun. And despite the bumps along the way, it was a road they'd walk together, hand in hand.

The End

(Excerpt- Through Thick and Thin, Ridgeview Book 3)

Kendrea eagerly walked into the semi-dark interior of Howie's Pub. She was going to have a meeting with her friend Tiffany about catering for her sister Kenny's wedding, and afterward, she was going to have dinner with Thomas. He told her to meet him here; he had something important to ask her. They were hanging out more often than usual these days, and she was quite inexplicably growing more and more attracted to him.

It was baffling. He was the same old Thomas, her chubby friend from high school who could make her laugh through tears, her favorite pal. What had changed? Why was she suddenly seeing him in a different light this past year?

It was that date to the Chamber of Commerce dinner. Thomas had kissed her when he dropped her home. She laughed it off, but that kiss had kept her up that night. She had never been kissed like that before. Thinking about it, she still got tremors in her lower body.

And suddenly Thomas Sterling, her overweight friend, who was also her stepbrother since their parents had gotten married five years ago, was now the star of all her fantasies.

She was completely thrown by her feelings. Kendrea had always valued their friendship—solid, unshakable, built on years of trust and shared memories. But now, every time Thomas was near, her pulse raced, and she couldn't ignore how her gaze lingered on him a little longer than it should. Once a comforting sound, his laugh now seemed to light something deep within her.

She glanced around the pub, spotting Tiffany seated at a booth, scrolling through her phone. Kendrea waved and made her way over, brushing off the nervous energy buzzing under her skin. She needed to focus. Wedding catering came first, not the growing mess of emotions swirling around Thomas.

"Kenny better appreciate this," Tiffany said with a grin as Kendrea slid into the booth. "I've called in favors from my best vendors."

"You're the best," Kendrea said, flashing a smile, but her mind drifted to Thomas. What was so important that he wanted to discuss?

"Earth to Kendrea?" Tiffany's voice broke through her thoughts. "You okay? You look a little... distracted."

"Oh, sorry," Kendrea said quickly, shaking her head. "It had been a long day. Since I did Jairo and Audra's place, I have been getting offers left, right, and center. I am going to have to expand soon."

"That's a great problem to have," Tiffany said. "I have the same problem, too. After I catered their wedding, I had so many bookings, and it's all thanks to you."

"Don't mention it," Kendra said, "we look out for each other. So lets talk wedding."

"Okay," Tiffany nodded. They chit-chatted for a while. Kendrea took notes to double-check with her sister and Camden.

"So, who will you be bringing as your plus one?" Tiffany asked as they finished up their pressing business.

"No one," Kendrea fanned her off. "I haven't been in a relationship for close to a year."

Tiffany smiled. "And besides, Thomas will be there. What on earth do you see in the guy? Apart from his personality. He's huge. He looks like a supersized Pillsbury dough boy with curly, unruly hair, and can't you get him to shave? Good Lord, the beard adds another twenty pounds to him.

Kendrea stiffened at Tiffany's words, her smile fading. A surge of defensiveness rose in her chest, but she forced herself to keep her tone light. "Well, thankfully, I'm not shallow enough to judge someone by their size or beard length."

Tiffany's brows shot up. "Whoa, relax! I didn't mean to hit a nerve. I just... I guess I don't get it. You're drop-dead gorgeous, K. You could have any guy you want."

Kendrea offered a tight smile, the heat of annoyance simmering just below the surface. "Thomas is amazing, Tiff. He's kind, funny, dependable—more than I can say for most guys I've met."

Tiffany raised her hands in surrender. "Okay, okay, I get it. No judgment here. If he makes you happy, that's what matters." She paused, then added with a teasing grin, "But are you sure there's nothing going on? You're awfully quick to defend him."

Kendrea felt her cheeks warm, but she shook her head. "There's nothing going on. We're just... close."

"Uh-huh," Tiffany said, clearly unconvinced. "Well, if you ever want to talk about it, you know where to find me."

Before Kendrea could respond, Thomas walked into the pub and looked around. He was in a good mood, his rotund figure practically bristling with excitement.

He wore a navy shirt that looked as if it were about to burst around his belly, paired with his signature blue jeans. He had actually shaved his beard—thank goodness, it had not been doing him any favors.

He still had long hair, though, at least he had brushed it back and tied it in a ponytail. He was clearly a good-looking guy, even with the extra weight. If you squinted hard enough, you could see similarities to Will Demps, the half-Korean, half-Black NFL player turned model. They had similar facial features, in her biased opinion. Thomas had about the same genetic makeup—his mother was Korean, and his father was

Black Jamaican.

The same strong jawline, a bit of a cleft chin, and those dark, almond-shaped eyes that could melt you if you weren't careful. His features weren't as sharp, far from it, but the resemblance was enough that Kendrea had often caught herself daydreaming about the comparison—though, of course, she would never admit that aloud.

He caught sight of her and waved, his face lighting up with that trademark grin—the one that always made her heart skip just a little. It was a warm, genuine smile as if he was glad to see her, even when they were just hanging out casually.

She stood up, smoothing her hands over her jeans. "I'll see you later, Tiff. Thanks again for helping with the wedding."

"Sure thing," Tiffany said, eyeing her with a knowing smirk. "Have fun with Pillsbury."

Kendrea rolled her eyes but didn't respond. She met Thomas halfway across the pub, her pulse quickening as he smiled down at her.

"Hey, Kendrea," he said, his deep voice sending a shiver down her spine. "Hope I'm not interrupting. I assumed you guys would be done by now."

"We are done," she replied, her voice softer than she intended. "Ready for dinner?"

"Yeah, but, uh..." He hesitated, rubbing the back of his neck. "Can we talk first? There's something I've been meaning to ask you."

Kendrea's stomach flipped. "Sure," she said, gesturing to an empty table nearby. "What's on your mind?"

As they sat down, Thomas leaned forward, his expression uncharacteristically serious. "Kendrea, I've been meaning to tell you this, I can't keep it in any longer. I met someone. It's getting serious."

"What?" Kendrea frowned. "When? Who?"

Thomas chuckled. "Remember Amanda from high school?"

Kendrea's heart dropped into her stomach, and she forced herself to sit still, not letting her shock show. "Of course, I remember her. She was one of the girls who wouldn't give you the time of day. She and her friends used to teased you."

"But now she likes me. Like, really, really likes me," Thomas said, a hint of disbelief still in his voice. "She lives in the States, came out for my buddy Griffin's wedding, and we started chatting. Before you know it, we made a connection."

Kendrea blinked, her mind racing. She wanted to ask him a million questions: What did she do? Was she using him like so many others? As big as he was, that did not deter the girls from flocking to Thomas. He was wealthy, he drove a nice vehicle, and he was a sensitive soul. He usually fell for their sob stories until he found out they were using him. Then he would get depressed and complain to her about nobody loving him for who he was.

"I hope Amanda is not going to trample on your self-esteem like the others," Kendrea said.

"I doubt that," Thomas said. "Amanda is a health and fitness coach."

"She is?" Kendrea raised an eyebrow.

"Yup, certified, degreed, and runs her own business. She offered to move out here and be my coach for six months. She has a partner, a chef who will do all my meals."

"And you will pay her?" Kendrea asked skeptically.

"Yes, she's doing a service," Thomas was getting annoyed.

"How much?" Kendrea asked suspiciously.

"Enough," Thomas said shiftily. "And that's what I want to talk to you about."

"What?" Kendrea asked.

"I want her to stay at my Ridgeview house. I'm going to be there too."

"And you want me to decorate it for you and your new lady love," Kendrea sighed, "and your chef?"

"She's not my new lady love," Thomas said quickly. "We had a connection, that's all I said. You raced to conclusions. But you sound jealous, and I like that." He looked smug.

"I am not jealous," Kendrea snorted. I am just completely flabbergasted by how gullible you are with these women. Last year, it was Nicole. Remember her? She sent a recording to her friend saying she was sleeping with you because she wanted to milk you for all you had. This year, it's Amanda. Next year, it will be someone else."

Thomas sighed. "I'm twenty-six years old, an overweight guy with all the needs and desires of any normal male. The one woman that I want, above anyone else, has shoved me into the friend zone. What do you suggest I do, Kendrea? Live like a monk? Slink around the place and beg for scraps of your affection? No thanks. I'm tired of waiting around for something that's never going to happen."

Kendrea's heart skipped at his words, and for a moment, she didn't know how to respond. She'd always been there for Thomas—listening to him complain about his love life, encouraging him when he was down—but hearing him talk like this... it felt different. It stung.

"I didn't put you in the friend zone, Thomas," she scoffed at the idea. "We've always been friends. You were the one who decided to change the status quo a couple of months ago, after the Chamber of Commerce dinner and kissed me. Until then, I didn't even know you liked me like that. You were always chasing after one girl or another and telling me about them."

"To make you jealous!" Thomas said. "And you never got

the message!"

"I got the message when you kissed me," Kendrea said. "Admittedly, I liked it. I can't stop thinking about it. I was contemplating taking things further. I even thought this was what this wretched dinner was about. I thought we were finally going to clear the air, but instead, you're telling me that you've met someone with whom you have a connection again. I feel like a clown."

"Wait, hold up," Thomas said. "You're saying if there was no Amanda, you would seriously date me?"

"Yes! Maybe! I don't know," Kendrea growled. "I shouldn't even be telling you anything now that you have Amanda."

Thomas looked at her in shock. "Well, this adds a new spin to things. I was going to ask you to move in with us at Ridgeview and act as a buffer. I don't want to be blindsided again by someone out to use me. I thought you would be perfect to sniff things out. After all, you clocked Nicole from the beginning, and you can read people's intentions like a book. But in light of new revelations, maybe you don't want to help."

"I wouldn't say that," Kendrea said. "I've been dying to decorate one of those Ridgeview houses to my taste. I know you'll just have me doing whatever I want, so that's a plus."

Thomas nodded. "Please don't ask me anything about colors and whatnot. And you'll have to consult with Amanda about the gym. I told her I had a blank slate. She was excited about that."

"I am going to put Amanda and her chef in the staff suite," Kendrea said. "Is the chef male or female?"

"Female," Thomas replied. "They're a two-for-one deal. Amanda says she'll prepare delicious, nutritious meals."

"Okay, I'll do it. I'll move in for six months. When does Amanda want to start?"

"As soon as possible," Thomas said.

Discover Exclusive Offers and Be the First to Know!

If you haven't already, don't miss out on the opportunity to join my New Release Newsletter! Sign up today and become part of an exclusive community where you'll be among the first to hear about my latest book releases and take advantage of special prices.

Why join my mailing list?

Be the First: Get a head start and be the first to know when I release a new book.

Exclusive Discounts: Unlock special prices available only to subscribers. Enjoy limited time offers and save big on your favorite books.

Quick and Easy: Signing up takes less than 30 seconds.

To join, visit https://www.brenalbar.com/newsletter or scan the QR code below.

Thank you for your support, and happy reading!

Ridgeview Series

The Ridgeview series follows five couples on the Jamaican north coast in the luxurious community of Ridgeview. It explores their everyday struggles with careers, children, and family drama. Each book touches on love, marriage, and trust as the characters face challenges that test their relationships.

Ride or Die (Book 1)
Play For Keeps (Book 2)
Through Thick and Thin (Book 3)
Tried and True (Book 4)
Stay With You (Book 5)

Spice and Stone Series

Join three extraordinary girls—Cinnamon, Cayenne, and Sage—as they navigate the intricate flavors of life, love, and romance in the captivating Spice and Stone series.

Cinnamon (Book 1)
Cayenne (Book 2)
Sage (Book3)

The Crimson Hill Series

Where family drama, romance, and a touch of sci-fi blend seamlessly in the enchanting backdrop of a small town in Jamaica. Prepare to embark on an unforgettable journey as secrets unravel, passions ignite, and destinies intertwine.

The Wiley Brothers

Step into the world of the Wiley Brothers, where tragedy weaves an unbreakable bond and love becomes their guiding light. In this captivating series, follow the journey of six remarkable boys as they navigate the tumultuous path of growing up without parents, discovering love, and finding their place in a challenging world.

Between Brothers (Book 0)- How it all began…
For Pete's Sake (Book 1)- Preston's story.
Crossing Jordan (Book 2)-Jordan's story.
Fire and Walter (Book 3)- Walter's story.
The Perfect Guy (Book 4)-Guy's Story.
The Patience of a Saint (Book 5)- Saint's Story.
A Case of Love (Book 6)- Case's Story.

The Pryce Sisters

Follow the remarkable journey of the Pryce triplets as they navigate the complexities of growing up, discovering romance, and embracing the exhilarating challenges of the new adult years.

Baby For A Pryce- Book 1
Right Pryce Wrong Time – Book 2
Yours, For A Pryce- Book 3

The Jacksons

Prepare to be enthralled by the captivating saga of the Jackson family. In this gripping series, secrets unravel, paternity questions loom, and love blooms in the most unexpected corners.

Ace- Book 1
Deuce- Book 2
Trey- Book 3
Quade- Book 4

The Scarlett Series

Their patriarch died and unexpectedly left each of them a fortune. Watch as the Scarlett family navigate their way through the ups and downs of sudden wealth, family secrets, and the complicated dynamics of their relationships.

Scarlett Baby (Book 1)
Scarlett Sinner (Book 2)
Scarlett Secret (Book 3)
Scarlett Love (Book 4)
Scarlett Promise (Book 5)
Scarlett Bride (Book 6)
Scarlett Heart (Book 7)

Magnolia Sisters

They were the rejects. The worst of the lot, they grew up in a girl's home together and formed sisterly bonds. Each book in the series tells the story of a different girl and the unique struggles and triumphs she faces along the way. With themes of friendship, forgiveness, and the power of love, the "Magnolia Sisters" series is a heartwarming and inspiring read that you won't want to put down.

Dear Mystery Guy- Book 1
Bad Girl Blues- Book 2
Her Mistaken Dream- Book 3
Just Like Yesterday – Book 4

New Song Series

A group of friends started out as a church band, see how each of them navigate their personal and professional lives while staying true to their faith and facing challenges along the way. With themes of forgiveness, redemption, and second chances, the New Song Series is a captivating read for anyone who enjoys heartwarming stories of love and faith.

Going Solo- Book 1
Duet on Fire- Book 2
Tangled Chords- Book 3
Broken Harmony- Book 4
A Past Refrain- Book 5
Perfect Melody- Book 6

The Bancrofts

The Bancroft family delves into the inner workings of academia and the high-stakes world of university politics. The family wrestles with the pressures of maintaining their family's legacy, they must confront their own demons and navigate the complex relationships that bind them together. From unexpected love affairs and betrayals to scandals and secrets that threaten to tear them apart, this is a series that will keep you captivated until the very end.

Homely Girl- Book 0
Saving Face- Book 1
Tattered Tiara- Book 2
Private Dancer- Book 3
Goodbye Lonely- Book 4
Practice Run- Book 5
Sense of Rumor- Book 6
A Younger Man- Book 7
Just To See Her- Book 8

Three Rivers Series

Three Rivers Series, a captivating tale of love, redemption, and second chances set in a picturesque community in St. Ann's Bay, Jamaica.

Private Sins- Book 1
Loving Mr. Wright- Book 2
Unholy Matrimony- Book 3
If It Ain't Broke- Book 4

The Resetter Series

The Resetter Series takes a look at a rare kind of person, a person who can travel back in time, but they only have one chance to get things right if they go back! With themes of second chances, changing the past and the power of love, the resetters series is a captivating time travel romance that many readers have described as a page turner.

Never Too Late- Book 1
Never Say Never- Book 2
Now or Never- Book 3
Almost Never- Book 4

On the Rebound Series

Experience the gripping and emotionally charged On the Rebound series, where love, betrayal, and redemption collide in a whirlwind of passion and secrets. Brace yourself for a journey filled with drama, cheating scandals, DNA questions, and ultimately, the power of second chances and finding love again.

On the Rebound- Book 1
On the Rebound Book 2

Standalone Books

Full Circle- After graduating from university, Diana wanted to return to Jamaica to find her siblings. What she didn't foresee was that she would meet Robert Cassidy and that both their pasts would be intertwined, and that disturbing questions would pop up about their parentage just when they were getting close.

After the End- Torn between two lovers. Colleen married her high school sweetheart, Isaiah, hoping that they would live happily ever after, but life intruded, and Isaiah disappeared at sea. She found work with the rich and handsome Enrique Lopez as a housekeeper and realized that she couldn't keep him at arm's length.

Love Triangle: Three Sides to the Story- George, the husband. Marie, the wife, and Karen-the mistress. They all get to tell their side of the story.

New Beginnings- Inner-city girl Geneva was offered an opportunity of a lifetime when she learned that her 'real' father was a wealthy man. Her decision to live up-town meant she had to leave Froggie, her 'ghetto don,' behind. She also found herself battling with her stepmother and battling her emotions for Justin, a suave up-towner.

The Preacher and the Prostitute- Prostitution and the clergy don't mix. Tell that to ex-prostitute Maribel, who finds herself in love with the Pastor at her church. Can an ex-prostitute and a pastor have a future together?

Historical Fiction

You won't want to miss out on these two captivating reads!

"The Pull of Freedom" tells the story of a slave family and their desperate struggle for freedom in Jamaica's colonial era. Follow the journey of these brave individuals as they fight for their right to be free, facing danger, heartbreak, and unimaginable obstacles along the way.

"The Empty Hammock" takes readers on a journey through time, as a modern woman finds herself transported back to the Taino era of Jamaica's history. Experience the wonder and mystery of this ancient culture through her eyes, as she learns about their traditions, beliefs, and way of life. With richly drawn characters and a beautifully realized setting, "The Empty Hammock" is a must-read for anyone who loves historical fiction that transports them to another time and place.

Short Story Collections

Di Taxi Ride and Other Stories- Funny stories about Jamaican life to make you laugh.